CCW

&

THE GAME CHANGER

CCW

&

THE GAME CHANGER

Kierra Smith

iUniverse LLC
Bloomington

CCW & THE GAME CHANGER

iUniverse books may be ordered through booksellers or by contacting:

iUniverse LLC
1663 Liberty Drive
Bloomington, IN 47403
www.iuniverse.com
1-800-Authors (1-800-288-4677)

ISBN: 978-1-4917-2833-8 (sc)
ISBN: 978-1-4917-2834-5 (e)

Library of Congress Control Number: 2014904479

Printed in the United States of America.

iUniverse rev. date: 03/10/2014

Acknowledgments

First, I'd like to Thank God for holding on to me when I wanted to let go and for every storm that has brought me to this moment of sunshine.

Secondly, to my husband Deloni and my parents Ken & LaJuana: for their never-ending encouragement and support to explore and pursue my passion for writing.

Also, to every friend and family member that has endured my grumbling, complaining, crying and insanity during this process.

And last, but not least to my Anonymous Muse: thank you for being what I needed, when I needed it most.

The biggest coward is a man who awakens a woman's love with no intention of loving her.
—Bob Marley

PROLOGUE

The bright headlights of the black 760 Li BMW beamed as it pulled into the driveway of the three story brick home with the detached garage. The sun was setting and the sky that was once filled with bright clouds was slowly turning into an array of pale orange lines. Before the vehicle could come to a complete stop, the deliciously shaped figure slid into the passenger side that was designated for her. Using her freshly manicured hand to clasp the chrome handle of the interior door, she closed it gently and secured the lock.

The sweet scent of her perfume filled the vents and temporarily seduced the driver as she conformed to the firmness of her chair. Leaning into him, she rested her hand upon his as it clung to the driver's gear shift. Slowly, she allowed her lips to swipe the flesh of his earlobe as she whispered, "What can I do for you honey?"

The man to her left was dressed in a Cashmere crème sweater with a pair of black slacks that accented his Ferragamo shoes. He had always enjoyed her presence, but his dilemma had temporarily disabled the powers that she possessed over him. He looked tensed and distressed when he replied, "I need to find a distraction, preferably someone who is good at deception without making the situation complicated and stressful."

Shifting her attention out of the passenger side window and allowing her mind to drift briefly. She had a suggestion, but paused before making the next statement. "I have someone with a particular set of skills that are more advanced than mine, but he's been out of the game for a while."

"So if he's in hibernation, what good is he going to do for me?" He was failing to balance his irritation and he wasn't in the mood to deal with stupidity.

Squeezing the grip that she had on his hand and trying to calm his rising temper, the mystery woman affirmed. "I'm certain that he would be willing to come out of retirement for the right price!"

"Money is no object, you know that!" He glanced at her and saw the plan, formulating in her eyes.

She smiled at his cockiness and informed, "I can give you the name and address of where the distraction can be located, but the rest is up to you!" Kissing his cheek, she slipped out of the luxury vehicle as quickly as she had come, leaving behind the silhouette of her small and petite frame!

Three days later

Distorted, confused and damp, Ice woke in a dark room with a crook in his neck and a nagging headache that almost crippled him. He was unaware of where he was, the events that had taken place and how he had gotten there. There were leaking pipes with rust surrounding the exterior and rotted cement that gave him the impression of an abandoned building or empty warehouse. For the scenery, he would have expected the stench to be revolting and close to death, but it smelled of clean linen. He wasn't sure if his senses could withstand further assault than the intensity his pounding headache had conjured. Within seconds, the lights switched on and half a dozen pair of legs descended the stairs.

Ice shifted in his chair, trying to stabilize his heart rate in order to remain calm. He'd come from the streets, where he had survived the worst and he refused to die begging and pleading. His self-respect and dignity meant everything to him and he wasn't going to allow anyone to snatch it. Ice had done so much in his lifetime and he had caused more mischief, grief and trouble than a hurricane or tornado on the loose. He was known for the torturous teasing and terrorizing towards all that were within his reach.

As the six men stood at attention, there was one with a medium build and probably the same height as Ice. He was different than the rest, his style was impeccable and it screamed money, but it was the shimmer of excitement in his eyes that alarmed Ice. The man stepped forward and sized Ice up from crown of his head to the soles of his feet. Turning towards that other men that surrounded him, he chuckled. "Damn Dawg, did you have to hit him in the face?"

"Boss I didn't hit him, he fell once I injected the shot and no one caught him!" Another man answered.

The Boss, who seemed to have authorized this small gathering, turned his focus back to Ice who was sitting in the chair. "You don't know me, but I am well aware of who you are and your position within my company. But, this assignment is unrelated to your current job description because what I need from you appeals more to your past expertise."

Narrowing his gaze and lifting his eyes to stare at the "Boss," Ice spoke. "I'm not sure I understand your request or how I could be of assistance to you. As far as I'm concerned, you have the wrong mothafucka and I sincerely need you to miss me with the bullshit."

The Boss turned in the direction of his heavily armed entourage, "I like him. He's going to be a perfect match because he won't give up easily." Redirecting his attention back to his guest in the chair, "May I call you Ice? That is what you were referred to as in your former life, correct?" Unnerved by the silence of his guest, the Boss motioned for one of the men to pass the duffle bag that Ice hadn't noticed before.

With a full blown headache, Ice was utilizing three senses instead of five to block out the pain. Tossing the bag between Ice's legs, the Boss continued with the mission at hand. "There is a half of million dollars in this bag and the assignment won't require you to do anything illegal. But, I need to know now if you are on board and that I can count on you to see this through!"

Ice closed his eyes for a moment to think; he hadn't dabbled in this lifestyle in years. It had almost over-taken him and he had vowed that he would never return. He didn't want to do it, but who couldn't use $500,000.00? Ice may have been making a deal with the devil, but he was praying to God to keep his soul! "ALRIGHT, I'LL DO IT, COUNT ME IN!"

PART 1

The Beginning of the End

CHAPTER 1

March 22, 2013

*W*ith twenty minutes left of her work day, Carla straightened up her desk and put her possessions in their perspective places. She couldn't stand to have papers everywhere and dust as thick as moth balls accumulating in the corners of her desk. It had been five months since the last time she spent time out of the office and she didn't want to return to a work space filled with clutter.

This time her vacation would be different because it would be for pleasure instead of business. After the last trip, Carla hadn't taken the time to lick her wounds, find peace in her mind nor mend her heart. She had promised to take the next month and revitalize herself, get some fresh air and heal. Never in a million years, could she imagine finding earth shaking, heart pounding, muscle clenching, tear jerking love and then have it walk out the door.

It wasn't until after everything was all said and done that she realized, she hadn't known Joshua at all. But, that didn't deter the emotional turmoil that Carla suffered on a regular basis. At times, she allowed her mind to capture flashback moments on what she thought was mutual love and respect between the two of them. But, he was completely protective over his world and had only allowed her to enter so far before shutting down completely.

Just before the New Year, Carla had returned back to counseling to work out some of the emotions that she battled constantly. Before then, she hadn't seen her therapist since her previous situation, so she was due for a purging of the soul.

In December of 2012, Carla walked into the therapist's office and sat in the chair while Dr. Kelly Smith removed her glasses from over the rim of her nose and asked. "Who hurt you? Tell me who they are and I'll break their knee caps. I see it all in your eyes!"

Carla enjoyed sessions with the doctor because she was animated and relatable, so she dismissed the idea of lying to her. Dr. Smith had revealed in her diagnosis that Carla was grieving the loss of the relationship and that nothing, but time could heal her. Amazed and comforted by the fact that her therapist had offered to call the man who had broken her heart, but unprepared for the revelation that came from the doctor's next question.

"How long has it been since Joshua's talked to you?" Dr. Smith began to pry.

"Two months!" Carla calculated.

Sinking back in her chair as if she were mowing over the words in her mind, the doctor continued. "If he hasn't spoken to you in several months Carla, then the truth is he doesn't want to be bothered!"

That particular truth had remained with Carla for the last couple of months. Whenever she missed Joshua or wanted to cry, she remembered that piece of reality that her counselor offered. Love was an action word, so if Joshua had truly loved her, then he wouldn't have left. Or at least, he would have reached out to her within the last five months. However, Carla hadn't spoken to Joshua and he had made sure that she couldn't reach out to him.

Pulling her thoughts from the flashback and forward to the present, Carla gathered the belongings that she would need for her vacation. She slipped the Michael Kors shoes that matched her suit perfectly on her feet and locked the office door as she reached the exit. Carla used her badge to punch out for the day while wishing farewells to Security when she noticed the figure seated to her left.

It felt as if someone had knocked the wind out of her chest and for a moment time stood still and she was convinced that her soul had temporarily left her body. If it weren't for the unexpected tears that escaped down her cheeks, dragging her back to reality, she would have been certain that she'd died and gone to hell. Carla was unsure of where the emotions had surfaced from and oblivious that they continued to linger after all of this time.

Joshua stood when he saw Carla from the waiting area and walked towards where she stood frozen in place and he whispered. "Sug."

Snapping out of the trance and stepping back as if he spit on her, "Sug?"

"CeCe." He corrected, knowing that she wouldn't be happy to see him after five months of silence.

"CeCe?" After a pause, she proceeded. "I'm not sure what world or black hole you crawled out of." Whispering harshly. "But you might as well return because my name is Carla Camille Williams."

"Carla. CeCe. Babe. Sug. Mami'." He pronounced and paused after every word to make sure the passion was heard in every endearment. "I'm sorry." Joshua reached out to wipe the tears that had fallen from her eyes.

But, Carla caught his hand mid-air before he could touch her. "Don't be sorry, its old news and I'm good." As they walked out of the Serenity Branch of Michigan towards her vehicle that was housed within the parking lot, Joshua was close on her heels.

"You have every right to be upset, hurt and angry, I owe you an explanation!"

She spun around to face him. "You don't owe me shit, we're good, it's been five months and I'm over it!" Carla continued in the route towards her vehicle again.

"Carla would you wait a minute? Let me explain, please. I Love You and that's why I'm here!"

Stopping in her tracks and whirling around again. "You love me? If that was your version of love, I would despise seeing how you show your affection towards someone whom you hate."

"Carla, I was scared, I didn't know how to tell you or how you would react and for the first time in my life, I didn't want to lose someone. I didn't want you to regret me or regret us!"

"Well, that's definitely too late, nothing you could have said would have made me run. I loved you; you gave me peace and restored everything that I thought had died inside of me. Joshua, you made me smile and you breathed life into me." Pausing to make her point and allowing her features to harden. "Right before you walked away taking it all with you."

The tears had magically returned causing Carla's voice to crack. "So it's unfortunate for you and what you claim happened, but you're going to have to kiss my ass on this one." She turned and resumed her pace trying to get to her truck and away from him because slowly the barrier she had built was dissipating in his presence.

Joshua reached out and grabbed her arm and she tried to pull away, but he tightened his hold and moved closer. He could feel her trembling as he pressed his forehead against hers and took a deep breath. "Sug. Babe. Carla Camille." He felt her lips curve upward into a sadistic smile. "Agree to spend the day with me tomorrow, we'll keep it light and I'll explain, okay?"

She didn't respond.

Joshua continued despite Carla's silence. "Your feelings are raw; you won't be rational with me right now and you're too emotional at the moment Babe. I'll come get you from your house in the morning, we'll have breakfast at my hotel and I'll explain."

Carla still refused to respond. She didn't trust her words around him. He made her resistance lapse and her walls crumble with every plea and confession.

His hands fell to her waist and he pressed his lips on hers, "I missed you, Sug." Breaking the connection, Joshua walked away.

Carla didn't remember walking to the car; driving home, walking upstairs to her bedroom or lying across the bed. A part of her was numb and she didn't know what to think or how to feel and every emotion that was buried after five months of searching for "WHY" had resurfaced.

Tears pooled her eyes and spilled down her cheeks and before Carla was able to control or contain it, she was weeping and sobbing. It was irritating, mind boggling and exhausting trying to fathom the concept of how one man in a three month time span had turned her world upside down.

Evening—March 22, 2013

The loud noise jolted her upward; head hurting, heart pounding wildly against her chest, Carla was ignorant to the fact that she had fallen asleep. Her eyes weren't completely open and she felt groggy, when the noise went off again. "OMGosh, it's the damn doorbell." She whispered, "I'm in no condition or head space for company." Glancing at the clock, it read **7:00pm,** guessing that she hadn't slept long when the door bell rang again, slowly shifting her into action.

Squinting through the peephole and breathing a sigh of relief that Carla didn't realize she had been holding as she swung open the door. Refusing to waste any time beating around the bush, she lit into her friend with a hint of genuine animosity. "Ky don't show up at my house, ringing my door bell like you're the police." Her smile disappeared when Kylie didn't respond and her expression conveyed something was seriously wrong. "What's wrong with you?" Carla asked concerned.

"No, what's wrong with you?" Kylie responded.

"Nothing, I'm fine, why do you ask that?"

"No, right now, you're a liar; your eyes are blood shot red, your voice sounds as if you just finished crying and it took you forever to get to the door. Your hair looks as if you just had raunchy sex and to top it off, I had a vision of you standing with a man that I have never seen before about three hours ago. So again I ask, what's the matter with you?"

Carla walked away from the door allowing Kylie to pass over the threshold of the house, Carla headed in the direction of the living room and left Kylie to shut and lock the storm door. She landed on the couch silently, knowing deep down inside she was going to have to lay down her burdens and come clean. Kylie was Carla's spiritual partner, confidant, intercessor, warrior, visionary and her sister-friend; so if she had a vision it was time for Carla to unlock and unload.

"Don't get quiet, it's in your eyes and it's all over your face." Kylie interrupted Carla's private thoughts.

"It's Sug." Carla sighed, "He's here."

"Who is Sug?"

"The devil." Carla tried giving Kylie a blank stare to drive the response home, but could only smack her lips when Kylie didn't back down or acknowledge the comment. "It's the older guy that I entertained while on that job assignment in Chicago."

"Why haven't I heard of him until now?"

"Well Ky, the way my pride is set up, I was too embarrassed and ashamed to mention it. I returned home feeling stupid, vulnerable and naïve and I figured if no one knew, then I could pretend that nothing happened. It made it easier to keep it to myself." Carla shrugged her shoulders and rested her head on the pillow that accessorized the couch.

Kylie's curiosity was peeked, "Kept what to yourself?"

"Him!" Carla responded flatly.

"Well since you're in the mood to play word games, I have a couple hours before the boys return home from basketball practice so you can go ahead and spit it out."

Carla sat there mute.

Running out of patience, Kylie urged, "All of it." In the tone that conveyed she was a mother of two teenage boys and she was not to be played with or mishandled because of her petite size.

Exhausted, emotional and confused, Carla took a deep breath. She closed her eyes and allowed her mouth to speak the words that her mind recalled five months earlier.

Chapter 2

August 13, 2012

*E*arly Monday morning, Carla walked into work as the sun peeked from behind the clouds and the birds chirped lightly on the window sill. She retrieved her messages from Porsha, the department's secretary and was informed that the CEO wanted to meet with all staff at 9am. Carla rendered a tight smile, turned and headed towards her office.

When Carla entered her sanctuary, she shut the door and sat behind the desk. She briefly allowed her mind to wonder what Jeff wanted to address on a Monday morning. *Hell, the toothpaste was barely rinsed out of my mouth good and they wanted to conduct a meeting?* Carla was praying that it didn't involve any heavy thinking because she was going to need at least another two hours and some breakfast before thinking was added to her agenda. It was 8am and Carla acknowledged that she had one hour to get her Mabel Simmons (Madea) mentality in check and step into the role as a professional and head trainer for the company.

At 8:55am, Porsha buzzed thru Carla's line to let her know that everyone was beginning to file into the conference room. Carla simultaneously began logging off the computer, grabbing a pad and pen and heading in the direction of the door. Recognizing that she was the last person to enter the room, Carla squeezed next to the lady with oversized reading frames. The lady had bi-focal lenses and a *Technology Help Desk* logo printed on her badge. On her left, was the nerd from the mail room, who had a fetish for digging in his nose when he believed no one was watching him. He incessantly gave the term, mail carrier, a new definition. The reason why this was the only seat available in the whole damn conference room was clearly evident.

"Relax Madea," she mused to herself!

As if on cue Jeff began the meeting.

"As everyone knows, things have changed and shifted the last couple of weeks without much explanation. Today, all will be revealed. Serenity has taken over Humility Bank of Chicago. The change is effective immediately, no one's job is at risk, but some will be relocated to different departments within the offices to assist and support. We want to ensure that the transition of one corporation merging with another is as smooth as possible."

"Carla," Jeff called out.

Her pen froze mid sentence as she lifted her head to meet his direct stare.

"Yes Jeff?" She replied.

Jeff went on to say. "We have decided that it would be best to have the head trainers of each corporation collaborate and work together. We want you to compare and contrast ideas and suggestions for team building. Also, we are seeking the reconstruction of protocols, policies and procedures to ensure that Humility's employees are completely trained on how we conduct business. In view of the fact that they are a smaller corporation it shouldn't be difficult for you to manage."

Coming out of a trance, Carla found her voice. "So who is the other person and when will I meet her?"

"Umm, well she is actually a "HE" and his name is Joshua Williams, but I want you to be gentle with him, welcoming almost." Jeff smirked.

"Why? Is he still on the bottle with a hint of Similac on his breath?" Carla joked as she gathered laughter from her audience.

"NO." Everyone turned their attention to the door. "I do believe that I have moved on to solid table foods at this stage in my career." Joshua continued with a smirk of pleasure as he registered Carla's shock, whose back just so happened to be positioned towards the door.

Jeff interjected, "I do believe the two of you will get along just fine." He proceeded and resumed his attention to the others present in the room. "Everyone else will receive additional instructions and/or partners via email if a change is required of you. If there aren't any questions, comments or concerns, feel free to fully utilize the open door policy, just remember to knock first."

Snickers of laughter and light conversation followed Jeff's last comment, lifting the mood a bit as morning began to glide into high noon.

"Alright, this meeting is adjourned until new information is retrieved and approved for disclosure. Have a great and productive day." Jeff concluded while nodding at Carla and Joshua to remain while the others gathered their materials to exit.

Carla glanced in Joshua's direction only to find that he was already staring at her. She had waited for her moment to size him up completely. He was a brown skinned 6'5" giant with a medium build and muscular shoulders. His combination of salt and pepper hair was smooth and wavy with a neatly trimmed mustache and goatee. The texture told Carla that Joshua was of more than African descent, but the pair of deep and dark penetrating black eyes is what held her captive. The pull that she felt when staring into his gaze, left her curious as to what he hid behind them.

Carla could recall her father telling her that no one's eyes were actually black, just dark brown, but maybe this character was the exception because his eyes were definitely black. They made her feel as if she were on the set of an episode of Charmed and he was a demon that the charmed ones were assigned to vanquish. She shook off the unwelcomed vision and tried to redirect her focus.

Jeff interrupted her thought process by sliding back into conversation. "Carla, Joshua flew in this morning to take a tour of our facility and observe your day to day operations. Since you don't currently have any training classes, I'm sure you can improvise and allot him two days of shadowing." Jeff expected Carla to compare and contrast how the two companies differed and where they could split and share some responsibility to ultimately eliminate overload.

Not giving Carla or Joshua an opportunity to comment on the request, Jeff carried on with the one sided dialogue. "Also, I know you weren't given much notice Carla, but the Board of Directors in Serenity concluded that it would be best for you to spend the next forty-five to ninety days at the Humility Branch Office Headquarters."

Carla processed the request with her right eyebrow lifted, "Okay, so where is the headquarters located?"

Jeff looked at Joshua and nodded. Clearing his throat, Joshua answered, "Headquarters is located in Chicago, Illinois."

"And how much time are you giving me to pack and head to Chicago?" Carla pouted while turning her attention back to Jeff.

Jeff confirmed, "You will have the next forty-eight hours starting from today while Joshua is shadowing. You two will leave Wednesday evening or Thursday morning and Joshua will accompany you on the drive. Unfortunately, we weren't able to secure you a furnished apartment, but we have provided a furnished hotel suite with a full kitchen for the next forty-five to ninety days. Or until we have collaborated trainings and policies that are in place and active."

"Okay, is that all?" Carla interjected.

"Do you have any objections?" Jeff asked concerned since Carla hadn't put up a fight, had a melt down or started any hysterics.

"Not at this time." She grumbled, shifting her attention back to her belongings that she brought to the meeting. Carla stood and turned towards the doors, she neglected to signal Joshua to join her because she could sense that he was already following.

Joshua took Carla's gesture of gathering her pad and paper as their key to exit and since they would be working together, it was in his interest to follow her lead. Her mouth didn't say what her eyes conveyed, but he understood this was her show and he would allow her to perform. Joshua was a no-nonsense, relaxed low-key kind of guy. He prided himself on controlling his emotions, so for the next two days he had nothing, but time.

As they entered Carla's office she continued the routine as if he wasn't there. She had taken off her shoes, climbed into the chair with one foot tucked underneath her bottom while the other foot dangled on the floor. Speaking only to ask Joshua to close the door behind him and extending a polite thank you.

Moments later Carla began to rant, "Joshua, I was briefed about this transition a month or so ago, but didn't expect it to happen so quickly. Please have a seat and make yourself comfortable, I apologize that my friendliness has taken a temporary leave of absence. I was definitely unaware of you and I joining forces and moving to Chicago for the time being. So excuse my enthusiasm to desert my perfectly cozy townhome for a hotel, where I don't know anyone." Carla tried to explain as calmly as possible, but failed to hide the sarcasm.

Joshua smirked, rendering a chuckle. "Thank you and I apologize for any inconvenience on my part. But, since this will be collaboration and not a dictatorship, I look forward to easing all of your worries and carrying Humility's weight the next couple of days. I am known as *The King* around my parts and I have no problem sharing my throne with you as the *Queen*. And you won't be alone; you'll have me, feel free to call me Jay instead of Joshua." He licked his lips imitating LL *Cool J* and clasped his hands together in the shape of a pyramid.

Matching his sly smile and showing off the dimple in her right cheek, Carla was flattered by his charm that hid a hint of cynicism. "I'll definitely share the throne with you, taking into consideration all of that cockiness you seem to possess. I'm certain you're going to need me to help balance you out."

Carla took Joshua's smirk as a silent agreement that he was just as intrigued about this partnership as she was. "Okay King, do you have any suggestions thus far on how to make this a smooth transition?"

"A few," Joshua countered. "But I would rather get to know you a little better, to relieve any tension, break the ice and create the space for a peaceful and loving work environment."

Carla's burst of laughter caused her to almost fall out of her chair, she knew she was a little dramatic, but she had to match his performance. "You just don't stop do you? Are you trying to win me over or hit on me?"

"Neither," Joshua confirmed. "I just want you to put your claws away and calm the lioness that's underneath your wardrobe, hidden behind your diplomas and concealed in that half smile you're offering me. I'm not here to complicate your job, steal your job or become the competition. I would like to work with you in harmony to bring a force between both entities compounding a mega unit that's on one accord."

Shocked at his candor Carla recoiled, "For starters, I'm not the least bit worried about you evicting me from my position and the lioness as you refer to it, is calm and in hibernation currently."

Silently, Carla was resolved that she liked his swag and his tongue conveyed a lot, but his eyes didn't communicate what his mouth had offered. Her curiosity was peeked and the tension could be felt in the room, but it had nothing to do with collaborating or unifying two banks. Maybe it was the sway in his voice with a bit of southern drawl, the confidence of his stride and the no-nonsense grasp in his eyes. Either way, Joshua Williams definitely had her attention.

Three hours had gone by with Carla showing Joshua safety guidelines, policies and procedures with him chiming in to give his expert opinion on how to expand or clarify the documents. Carla glanced at the clock that read 1:30pm, forcing her to call it quits.

"Okay, I don't know about you, but I could use some lunch, Jay!" Carla watched as Joshua glanced at his watch, hiding the amusement that formed across his face when she called him Jay instead of Joshua for the first time.

"I hadn't noticed that it was this late in the afternoon." He replied.

"I know, we were a bit caught up in revising the handbooks." Carla agreed.

Joshua stood from his leaning position over Carla's shoulder and walked around to sit in the chair that he claimed as his own when he first walked into her office. He couldn't help, but get caught up in the way that she smirked and smelled. "Okay, so what do you want for lunch? My treat!" He concluded.

"You don't have to buy my lunch, you're a guest here and whatever you want to eat, I'm content with it."

"So you're treating me to lunch?" Joshua asked.

"Not at all King, you can afford to purchase your own meal!" Carla corrected him.

Rather than debate with her, he figured he had plenty of time to crawl under the wall of stubbornness that she had constructed so for now he would oblige. "Some cheese pizza, chicken wings or salad would be fine or a fish sandwich from McDonald's is always convenient."

"Do you mind if we settle for McDonald's today and tomorrow evening after work we can go for that three course meal you're pushing for?"

"It's not that I'm pushing for anything, I don't eat a lot, but when I do eat, I don't mind indulging."

Leering at the Man's witty personality and quick comebacks, she resigned. "Okay, well let's get you something to eat so that we can try and finish the handbooks today, that way we can work on something else tomorrow."

Carla liked him and so far they worked well together. Joshua assembled his jacket onto his shoulders and zipped it to the center of his chest. He reached for the door of the office and propped it open as he extended his hand in front of him and bowed at the waist to gesture, "After you!"

CHAPTER 3

After a long day full of surprises, a bubble bath and a bottle of wine is what Carla needed because she was officially off of duty. Not only did they want her to go to another state and train, but the company wanted her to take up residence there for the next three months. If she were honest with herself, what was her real complaint besides being outside of her comfort zone? It's not as if she had a man or a family that the relocating would affect.

Why didn't she have a man? She often questioned herself; it wasn't as if educated, beautiful, plus size, successful, ambitious fertile women had gone out of style. There were plenty of men who were trying to knock down her door as well as the walls of her vagina, especially one in particular. The phone rang redirecting her thoughts.

"Hello!" Carla answered.

"Hey CeCe, what are you doing?" Morgan, Carla's best friend greeted on the other end of the phone. Their normal greetings ranged from a variety of things, the idea was if they thought it, then they said it and it was just as simple as that.

"Nothing just got in from work not too long ago, what's going on?"

"Oh nothing, I may need you to watch Skylar for a couple hours until Brandon gets off of work." Morgan stated.

Silence engulfed the line.

"Come on Fatty, it's only for a few hours." Morgan begged.

"Skylar is "Satan's little helper," with a smart mouth, large vocabulary and hundreds of questions for a six year old."

"She isn't shit, but a miniature you so I don't know why you're so upset about it. This is Gods way of torturing you because of all the hell your family and I have had to endure for the last twenty-eight years and for the hell that we are currently enduring and all the hell that is to come."

Carla exhaled so hard that you would have thought the doctor was giving her a checkup, "Skylar gets two hours of my time before my eyelids close and she's forced to watch herself."

Morgan's burst of laughter, prompted Carla to join in. It was their own private joke that Carla's version of babysitting was the kid actually watching him or herself anyway. She didn't have any children, her patience was short and she couldn't relate to them the way most people could. In Carla's sophomore year in college she changed her major from Elementary Education to Training and Development. She discovered that she loved and enjoyed to teach and impart knowledge, but she didn't like kids as much as she thought she had at one point.

"I need to tell you about my interesting day at work when you get here." Carla said dryly.

"Okay, I'll see you within the next hour CeCe." Morgan replied without acknowledging the lack of enthusiasm in Carla's statement.

Ending the call, Carla looked around the house and considered straightening up a bit, but there wasn't much to do and she wasn't in much of a mood. Her mind to clean flipped to the contents in her refrigerator to preoccupy

Skylar. Or Skylar would definitely entangle her in a drawn out conversation about her young life. Skylar's thoughts would drift from her friends at school, a program on television or capture Carla with a large word that she had collected and sealed in her vault that composed of her vocabulary.

Just as she was about to head for the kitchen the doorbell rang. Initially, she thought of just opening the door, but thought better to ask who it was. "Who is it?" Carla called out with one hand on the lock and the other gripping the door knob.

"It's Santa dummy, open the door." The person replied.

Giggling Carla already knew Morgan was the voice on the other side of the door. She unlocked the storm and screen door to let her friend of twenty years and god-daughter in the house.

Skylar jumped up. "Hi, Mama CeCe!"

"Hi Sky."

"Who else were you expecting?" Morgan blurted.

"I don't know maybe Santa Clause was getting an early start on presents this year because I damn sure deserve one."

"Is that right? Why is that?" Morgan asked.

"Because I was extremely calm, level-headed, silent and non-volatile today when my boss told me that he's shipping me off to Chicago. For the next forty-five to ninety days, I will instruct a training course for the company that we are currently merging with."

Morgan sat there with her mouth gapping open. "And you left the building standing?"

Carla could count on Morgan to brighten her day because she didn't have the average human being's personality and it was probably because she had the funniest parents that Carla had ever encountered. "The building is still intact and standing for now, but if this trip back-fires or if this old man turns out to be a real live asshole, then all bets are off!" There was a bit of laughter in Carla's voice.

"Umm, what old man CeCe?" Morgan lifted her eyebrow.

"The old man who is assigned to properly escort me into Chicago's Headquarters which also happens to be their head trainer from the merging company. His Government ID states Joshua Williams."

"So why is your slow ass calling him 'old man'?"

"Because even though his ass has swag, I can tell he is up in age by the salt and pepper hair and mustache."

"Well how old is he, exactly?"

"I don't know, I didn't ask him."

"Umph."

Carla was too tired to take this conversation any further. "Don't umph me, I'm leaving in two days, your man has two hours to come get your kid and then she's left to her own devices. Now get out and go to work." Carla rose to her feet and moved towards the door.

"Are you putting me out?" Morgan stood with her hand to her chest looking appalled.

"No ma'am, I'm escorting you to the door and helping you get to work on time, so I don't have to hear you blame me for your tardy behavior."

"That's a possibility." Turning in the direction of her daughter, Morgan called out. "Bye Sky."

"Bye Ma! Is my Daddy coming to get me or do I have to spend the night with Mama CeCe?"

"Oh no Suga," Carla interjected before Morgan could respond. "Your Daddy will be here in two hours, don't worry!"

"I'm not concerned, I was just asking, that's all." Skylar responded arrogantly to her Godmother.

Morgan filled the room with laughter, "You know what, I'm gone and yes Baby, your Daddy is coming to get you." Turning towards Carla, "Bye asshole."

"This six year old tells me she's not concerned, but I'm the asshole? Yea, I love you too Fatty, bye."

"I'll be back tomorrow to help you pack." Morgan said over her shoulder.

"K, have a good day!" Carla shut the door.

CHAPTER 4

The next morning at work, Carla didn't drag her feet as much since it was Tuesday. She was quite entertained by Mr. Williams and time sped by as they completed the handbooks that incorporated both companies. Carla's degree in Training and Development was utilized widely throughout the company crossing her job responsibilities when staff was short-handed or if departments needed additional support. But, she didn't mind at all, the more she kept her mind pre-occupied, the less trouble she stayed in.

By nature, as a January Capricorn it was easy for her to investigate and dig for information whether it was for others or herself, all she needed was motivation. She didn't grow up believing in horoscopes, but the signs never lied. Carla partially wondered if Joshua's zodiac sign could help explain the fire it lit under her. Clearing her thoughts, Carla picked up a little pace once she exited the elevators onto her floor where she found him standing at her office door.

"You're late!" Was how Joshua greeted her while he read the hands on his very expensive watch.

"I know, I'm sorry Jay, I didn't have your number to contact you. Besides it was only fifteen minutes, I figured since you're the King, you would find your way around this jungle if necessary."

"I see you got jokes early this morning!"

Carla giggled, "You play, joke, and smirk here and there, but you never smile. Why is that?"

"I don't smile much because there isn't a whole bunch to smile about." Joshua informed her.

"Well we will have to see what the Queen can do about that." Carla lowered her lids and turned her body to open the door for them to officially begin the day.

Joshua watched her walk ahead of him as she swayed towards her desk. He was memorized by the curve of her body and the attention she demanded in her stride. He noticed that Carla wasn't chunky or hefty, she was thick and proportioned. Thicker women weren't exactly what he longed for, but he would be lying to himself and the rest of the world, if he denied how beautiful and attractive she were.

Not to mention how her smile escalated the femininity that she possessed. Carla had to be about 5'7" with a coco brown complexion and skin that looked as soft as baby lotion. With eyes that were slanted and medium length eyelashes that accented them. Her lips weren't pouty, but more along the lines of plush! Carla wore her pressed and feathered hair down around her shoulders. It was gorgeous and as thick as a lion's mane, but flawless nonetheless. *Yes*, Joshua mused to himself, *Carla Williams was beautiful.*

Carla sashayed around her desk and pulled out the chair when she noticed that Joshua was staring at her. "What's the matter?"

Shifting out of his thoughts, he moved towards his chair, "Nothing, my mind drifted for a second."

"Drifted where?"

He paused and then decided to entertain her query, "To your hips and the curve of your shape. I was admiring how attractive you are."

Stuck to the spot next to the chair; casting her eyes downward and then lifting them to stare him dead in the face, "Oh!"

"Don't ask questions you don't want answers too, I'm much too old to lie."

Inwardly, Carla was grinning at the fact that Joshua opened the door for her to ask personal questions that ate at her curiosity from the day before. She had inherited a nosey nature, but she would never display it towards someone she'd just met. "Exactly how old are you?"

"Why? How old are you?"

A rupture of laughter sprang from her throat, "I definitely asked you first."

"Forty-five."

"Oh!"

"Oh? What does that mean?"

"It doesn't mean anything, I knew you were older, I just didn't know how old."

"You're only as old as you feel!"

"I mean you look good for your age, I wouldn't have guessed forty five years old."

"Okay, so how old are you?"

Carla didn't really want to tell him because of the seventeen year age difference, but when he raised his eyebrow after several long seconds of silence she conceded to tell him. "I. Am. Twenty-Eight. Years. Old." She couldn't help but enunciate each word very slowly because it was killing her to tell him. You would have thought that he ordered her to walk on hot coals the way she tried to elude his question.

Joshua could tell she didn't really want him to know, he wasn't sure if it gave him an advantage or not since he was older. He whistled to emphasize what he wanted to say, "That young huh? I have kids older than you."

"Don't be disrespectful," Carla countered. "And how old were you when you began having kids? Twelve?"

"Close, I was fifteen?"

It was Carla's turn to mimic the whistle that he gave her moments before to emphasize what she wanted to say. "That young huh?"

His laughter filled the room, shocking Carla into a stiff position as if someone had dropped some ice cubes down the back of her shirt. He caught himself once he saw the reaction on her face. "Yes, Babygirl I laugh, if it's funny enough and I think you're quite hilarious!!"

"Oh hell naw, don't you dare Babygirl me because you're old as hell and you have kids older than me. That does not negate the fact that I am grown in every sense and shape of the word as you noticed when I caught you staring!" Carla checked him.

The look on his face spoke volumes and Carla almost felt chastised, yet he hadn't opened his mouth to say one word. The glare of his eyes, showed the rage that flowed through his veins and it was verified in the twitching of his lips. Right then, in that very moment, not only did she wish she could take back what she said. But, it confirmed that the man with the deep dark eyes definitely had a dark side. The muscles in his jaw line clenched and Carla knew she had gone too far and struck a nerve.

"I didn't mean it as rude as it came out." Carla tried to fix her statement, but she had already perceived that it was much too late.

"It doesn't matter how you meant it, how about we just keep it professional from here on out? I believe I momentarily lost perspective of that." Joshua confessed.

Carla didn't know what to say, as swift as lightening; the playful Jay had gone back into hiding and allowing Joshua to resurface. The atmosphere had changed completely. The remainder of the morning was spent going through training materials without any side bar conversations.

By the afternoon Joshua's attitude hadn't returned back to humorous, he hadn't done anything close to smiling and his demeanor was absolutely professional. There weren't any sly remarks of how attractive Carla was or how nice of a shape she possessed. It was starting to bother her, there had to be something she could do to break the ice. At that moment he looked up from the training manual because Carla was positive he could feel her staring too long and had heard the war that was raging within her inner self.

"What?" He called out.

"Nothing, I was trying to find the words to soften your expression and cut the trepidation in the room. It's exhausting dodging the negative energy that's radiating off of your body. Are you that mad at me?"

"I'm not mad at all, but I won't tolerate you talking to me like I'm a sucka you bumped into on the street. I give respect and I expect nothing less than to have it reciprocated 100%."

Feeling reprimanded and humiliated, Carla whispered. "I sincerely apologize, I naturally talk hard, but I honestly didn't mean any harm, I'll try to be more conscious."

Joshua knew he had embarrassed her, it wasn't her tone or words, it was her eyes. He wondered if they were the windows to her soul. His forty five years on earth had taught him a few things, especially about women. But, as quickly as her vulnerability appeared, he watched her tuck it away with a blink of the eye. Before he could respond to her apology, she spoke again.

"For lunch, I think we should go our separate ways for a little bit of space. You know enough about the area to decide on a meal and you can GPS what you don't. Porsha, the department secretary can assist you with anything additional that you'll be in need of for the next forty to sixty minutes. We will be crowded in a car tomorrow evening so I'd rather not ruin my welcome with you."

Before he realized what happened, Carla was out of the door leaving him flabbergasted. "She's just as bi-polar as me." Joshua whispered underneath his breath. Had he just met his match?

When Carla returned from lunch an hour later Joshua was sitting in the same position that she left him in. He was as still as a statue with his hands folded in his lap and the expression on his face was throat cutting. Carla almost tripped on her feet upon entering the office because of how disturbed he looked.

Taking her time walking around the desk, she avoided eye contact because she didn't need those black eyes damning her soul to hell. She shouldn't have left the office the way she did for lunch, but she had to get some air, he was suffocating her with his overbearing presence.

As soon as she sat down, Joshua crossed the room, shut and then locked the office door. He walked towards Carla's chair and pulled it from under the desk with her still seated in it. He placed his arms on each arm of the chair and lowered his face over hers. And just as he was about to tear into her ass, he noticed the fear in her eyes.

"I'm not going to hurt you." He whispered. "But if this is going to work, we both need to relax. I think you're beautiful, but you're going to have to discard that stank ass attitude."

Giggling, "You think I have a stank ass attitude? You're the one that's bi-polar, you're Dr. Jekyll and Mr. Hyde without having to open your mouth. I feel like you're measuring me by some preconceived notion because I'm young with a little bit of authority and you're waiting for your moment to pounce and devour me."

"I'm not measuring you by anything, but that's an interesting concept. **BE YOU**, either I'll fuck with you or I won't!"

"Look at how you're talking to me, but I'm the one with the attitude?"

"Because you're not going to understand it if I say it any other way!" Joshua urged.

"Bullshit, I'm very intelligent, educated and competent, try me!"

Joshua's left jaw line twitched; she was getting under her skin and this was only day two, there was no way in the world he was going to make it forty-five to ninety days. He was convinced that the only way to calm and tame Carla would be to fuck the shit out of her. Plain and simple, but the reality was that he was looking forward to it; she was a missile waiting to be launched.

He was too quiet for comfort, but Carla needed to speak her peace. "I'm a handful, I understand that, if you can't handle that, then let me know now. Don't make me feel like I'm being checked and scolded every time I open my mouth."

"Do you want me to handle it?" Before he could filter his response, it was out of his mouth. But he wanted to know, he had to know and couldn't help but wonder if he were to put her in check with some dick, *could she handle that?*

There was no doubt that Carla understood his question and the underlining meaning, it had been close to five years since she had slept with a man. But there was no way in hell, she was about to open up and pour out her problems to this cocky son of a bitch.

"I can tell that you're at least thinking about it and I can tell that you're turned on." Joshua continued whispering. "We have forty-five to ninety days, so take your time." He leaned further down towards her chair and nibbled at her bottom lip. When Carla didn't pull away, he proceeded by slowly pulling it into his mouth, sucking and coaxing her tongue as they kissed with fluid movements as strategic and sexy as the tango.

He moved his right arm from the chair to her chin, tilting her head for complete access to her mouth as he tried to quench his new arising thirst. Joshua stroked the inside of her mouth with his tongue, all the while trailing his hand to the opening of her blouse. He recognized the change of pattern in her breathing when he fondled her hard nipples through the silk blouse. They were at attention and ready for his command, heightening the level of desire with every stroke of his fingers.

Carla knew that things were going too far, she was at work for Christ's sake. Using her limp hand, she pushed against his chest to get control of the situation. Joshua stepped back, partially remorseful and partially justified. "I'm sorry, that got out of hand." As he looked at Carla, her eyes remained cast downward because she couldn't allow him to see how much he affected her.

"You don't know if I'm married, single, dating or anything. How are you going to kiss me with no regard to that?"

"Why didn't you stop me?" He answered.

Carla didn't have an answer.

Joshua returned to his seat. "I do know that you're not actively seeing anyone, yesterday was our first day meeting, but I've seen you before. I may have inquired to Jeff about your relationship status."

"Hold on, you what?" Carla was two seconds from turning into the dragon lady. "And he voluntarily gave you the information?"

"No, what he said was, you were a lot to handle and that you aren't completely single, but you're married, but separated."

"He what?" Carla jumped out of the chair and landed on her feet. "What the fuck is going on around here? So y'all didn't have anything else to do with your time than to discuss my private affairs?" She was livid; Carla swore her nose was burning because she was breathing fire.

"Babygirl, calm down it wasn't like that at all." Joshua crept back towards her, pushing her against the desk that engulfed more than half of the office space. "Didn't we just discuss working on your attitude?" He placed his forehead against hers and enclosed his arms around her waist. He clasped her hips with his hands while concurrently biting his lower lip at the firmness of her body. Joshua imagined what her legs would feel like encircled around his waist as he slowly stroked in and out of her.

Weary with desire, Joshua focused in on Carla. "Carla, I'm not going to intentionally hurt you, so I need you to let me in a little." Pressing their bodies so close together that it felt as if they were breathing the same air. "You have to let your guard down some or there is no way we're going to be able to be professional around each other. It seems that the only time you're not going ham is when my lips are on yours or if I'm in your face, like now. But, unfortunately we cannot get any work done like this."

Carla silently agreed and Joshua let her go, she was too drained, it was almost as if all the tension and energy that she felt before had vanished. It was strange, but she felt better, almost relieved. She returned to her seat and professionalism re-entered the room, allowing them to go through the operating systems and PowerPoint slides that she would introduce to his teams once they arrived in Chicago.

When five o'clock came, Carla began packing up her personal effects. She knew he was watching her, but she didn't care, she felt open and had to escape him. Carla bent down, slipped on her shoes and turned to grab her jacket when Joshua grabbed her arms.

"It's called the transferring of energy."

"Huh?" Carla scrunched her face.

"What transpired between the two of us earlier . . ."

"Is that why I felt so calm?"

"Yes, I exchanged your energy for mine."

"How?"

"A little trick I learned."

"So you're not going to share it with me?"

"If I tell you, I'll have to kill you." This time Joshua smirked.

Carla returned his smirk. "I have to go, I'm a bit of a procrastinator in some areas of my life, so I'm not nearly ready to leave tomorrow!"

He reached over the desk and grabbed her cell phone. "Here's my number, call me if you need some help loading your luggage."

"Thanks, but I should be fine. I'll see you tomorrow, just lock my door behind you once you leave if you're not ready to go just yet."

"Okay, I'll see you tomorrow."

In route to her car, Carla felt her cell phone ringing from within her purse, retrieving it without much difficulty. She touched the screen on the side that said 'Answer' and greeted, "Hey Fatty, what's going on?"

"Nothing, I was calling to see what time you wanted me to come and help you start packing because I already know that your procrastinating ass hasn't done anything." Morgan insulted.

"Well right now, I feel like you're in my business and that insane theory may be slightly correct, but can you come tomorrow morning? I am too tired mentally to even think about it today!"

"Why have you met your match with the old man?" Morgan suspected.

"More than you know."

"What does that look like?"

"It looks like his sexy, old ass, locked me in my office and kissed me today!"

A gasp followed by laughter was Morgan's only response. "You bet not call me talking about he fucked the shit out of your hostile ass."

"And if I do I'm sure you're going to enjoy every detail." Carla basked at the thought of Joshua teasing and tasting her, all the while making herself slightly moist.

"I have my own man and my own sexcapades, I don't need to live through yours." Morgan stated with a thank you very much attitude.

"Well go ahead and give Brandon that junior that's he's been hinting at."

"See now you're in my business. Make me a damn Godmama like I did for you and we can discuss multiple children on my end."

"Hmmm Sweetheart, those chances may have died along with my marriage."

"Umph, see there you go, I'm done." Morgan laughed out loud.

"Good, I'll see you in the morning around 10am!"

"Wait, I thought you were supposed to work?"

"I'm not going, I haven't told them yet though, but I'll call off in the morning." Hearing her line beep, Carla looked at it and automatically knew that answering the call was going to be hard. "Fatty, I'll see you in the morning, my parents are calling and I forgot to tell them that I'm leaving."

"Oh shit, ok go ahead, I'll see you in the morning."

Clicking over to accept the other call, Carla answered. "Hi Daddy."

"Hi Baby, how are you? You've been quiet this week!"

"Daddy today is only Tuesday, we just talked over the weekend."

"Well it's nice to hear your voice either way."

Carla shook her head. "Daddy my job is transferring me to Chicago for a couple of months, tomorrow!"

"Tomorrow?"

"Yes, I just found out!"

"Are all expenses paid?"

"Of course they are." Carla couldn't help, but smile because her father was all about money, even at his age he still worked two full time jobs. If it didn't make dollars then it didn't make sense.

"Well that's all that matters, what time do you leave tomorrow?"

Huffing and puffing, Carla replied, "Sometime in the afternoon, since I won't be going into work, I'm going to pack my clothes instead."

"Well I'll call off too; I'll see you around 10am tomorrow."

"That sounds perfect Daddy and bring Mommy too." Carla knew that she needed to make more calls, but she wasn't given much of a time frame herself. She had to call her sisters, but she didn't want to hear their mouths. Although, Carla was confident that they would consider her relocation as a getaway for them to travel and visit.

"Okay Baby, see you tomorrow."

"I love you bye bye, Daddy."

Ending the call, Carla figured that she might as well get it out of the way. Dialing her youngest sister first and then her oldest sister; letting them know that they could come by the house in the morning for her farewell breakfast. Concluding the calls, Carla began to make preparations for breakfast. Since her family was coming, she might as well cater some food from the nearest Coney Island. Family was everything to Carla Camille Williams, they were her back bone.

CHAPTER 5

*W*hen Carla woke the next morning, she felt the bitter sweet tension arise with her. She had so much to do and not enough time, everything was happening so fast. She grabbed her cell phone, called her boss and then texted Joshua to let him know that he could come to her home this afternoon. Carla showered, made a call to Coney Island to confirm her previously placed order of; omelets, bacon, sausage, eggs, hash brown, toast, pancakes, jelly, butter, syrup and orange juice. She had always been a little self-conscious about what she ate because of how thickly proportioned she was, but today would be an exception.

One by one everyone filed in; it started with her bestfriend Morgan, her husband Brandon with her god-daughter Skylar in tow. Then moments later her youngest sister who was twenty-six years old, Chrissey strolled in. Ebony, was the oldest and two years, Carla's senior and her fiancé' Ivan with their daughter Amber, followed next. Her parents, Carlos, fifty-five years old and Eileen, fifty two, were the last ones to arrive, barring hugs and kisses.

It was rare everyone got together, but when they did the place was full of laughter and bliss. As everyone gathered around the table in the living, the conversation began with Morgan. "Fatty?" Morgan chimed, "Did you pack anything or do you expect me to help you pack after you've fed me all of this food?"

Carla smacked her lips. "I know you didn't think I fed y'all for free!"

Skylar chimed in. "Mama CeCe, I'm too little to help!"

"That information is incorrect, you ate didn't you?" Carla scolded.

"But I only ate a little," Skylar whined. Carla cut her eye and ignored Skylar's last comment; this was exactly why she didn't have any kids. When her Goddaughter went into whine mode then all bet's were off, indefinitely.

"Daddy?" Carla called.

"Yes CeCe?" Carlos replied.

"I need you to help me load the car once I get everything all packed away. You, Brandon and Ivan can watch television while we get everything organized, it shouldn't take long." Shifting her eyes to her soon to be brother in law; Ivan grinned and threw his hands up in a way that said it didn't matter. She knew that she could count on his easy going personality to help with whatever was necessary with no questions asked. "Great!" Carla exclaimed. As the women started in the direction of the stairs to the bedroom, the door bell rang.

Eileen asked her daughter, "Are you expecting more visitors to see you off?"

"No mom, I'm not, I wonder who it could be?" Moving towards the front door. Carla opened it and there he was on the other side and it seemed as if the entire room was focused on her in mere silence. "Hey Jay, I didn't expect to see you until later."

Before Joshua could respond, Chrissey cut in, "Ummm, who is this CeCe?" As Chrissey joined Carla at the door.

Bumping her sister out of the way while simultaneously opening the screen door for Joshua, he walked into the house greeting everyone. Carla decided to take the lead. "Everyone this is Jay aka Joshua and he is going to be accompanying me back to Chicago. I'm going to be training his team in-house."

Her father spoke first, "CeCe does Joshua have a last name?"

"It's the same as ours Daddy, its Williams!"

"I don't think he's related to us though!"

"Neither do I, Daddy." Carla giggled.

Lifting out of his chair, Carlos moved in the direction of where Joshua was standing and extended his hand. "I'm Pastor Carlos Williams". Carla couldn't help but snicker, she knew her father was using his calling and title to gain the upper hand. It was a tactic utilized to decipher the weak from the strong.

"CeCe what's so funny?" Carlos probed.

"Nothing at all, Daddy." Shifting the attention to everyone else she resumed introductions. "This is my mother Eileen, my youngest and bluntest sister, Chrissey. My oldest sister Ebony; Ebony's fiancé Ivan and my niece Amber. Over here," Carla extended her arm. "Is my best friend and Sister Morgan, her husband Brandon and my Goddaughter, Skylar."

After everyone exchanged pleasantries, Carla politely grabbed Joshua's hand and walked him to the kitchen where they had stored the leftovers from breakfast. When they were behind the swinging kitchen doors, she let him go. "Are you hungry?"

He was taken back by her hospitality, after yesterday's events and Carla not showing for work this morning, he was a little worried that he had been too forward with her. "Sure, what do you have?"

"What do you eat for breakfast?" She countered.

"Anything that's not pork related."

"Well. Ummm, you can have some pancakes, eggs and hash brown because you just eliminated the sausage and bacon."

"That's fine, I'll take it!" Joshua reached for a plate.

"Sure, as soon as you tell me how you got my address? I wasn't supposed to see you until later, so I wasn't going to send my address until later!" Carla informed him.

"Well Jeff—."

"Awe shit, here y'all go with this again!" Carla cut Joshua off in the middle of his sentence.

He bowed his head, bringing his hand over his mouth and imitating laughter. "Settle down!" When her only response was the rolling of her eyes, he continued. "I asked him for your address to come and assist you with packing. Is that alright with you Babygirl?"

"And here you go with this Babygirl mess again, if you haven't noticed, the guy in the living room is a damn good father and he raised one hell of a woman." Being that Carla was the middle child, she hated when people discarded her presence or accomplishments. She wasn't a baby and she wouldn't allow an older man to treat her as such. Carla would make sure that Joshua acknowledged her womanliness if he wanted to or not.

Joshua leaned in closer. "If you don't settle down and take some of that edge off your tone, I can assure you that you're going to be calling me Daddy in front of all those nice people in your living room!"

Carla couldn't help but sneer, she was turned on by his light threat. "Is that a threat Suga?" He didn't respond so she prompted further, "Daddy?" She paused to make sure that he caught the dual meaning.

Joshua shook his head and persisted to fix his plate, but faltered and turned in her direction. Before she could resist, his lips were on hers, but she didn't fight or pull back. Melting into him with her mouth inviting Joshua to invade his tongue pass her teeth and engage in a hunter and prey limbo. Carla elicited a slight moan from the intensity of the pursuit and Joshua knew he probably should have stopped, but he couldn't.

Putting his plate down beside her thigh, he allowed his hands to travel the length of her back, squeezing and cuffing every crease and fold. Oh, what he would give to have her ass plastered into him while gently stroking her from the back with her feet digging in the back of his thighs to balance. Closing the small distance between them Carla circled his neck with her arms and felt the erection in his pants, arousing her more. She squeezed her legs together to contain the fire brewing when he lifted her and placed her on the counter top. She spread her legs to allow him to settle between them as he slid her closer to the edge. Slanting Carla's frame to allow her to feel his bulge on her center as they roared the awareness of the restraint that was quickly unraveling.

"Carla Camille Williams!" Chrissey called out from the other side of the door. "Are you fixing the man a plate? Or are you in there serving him up?" Scaring the two of them out of the spell that made them forget where they were. Carla could hear Chrissey getting closer. Joshua stopped, pressed his forehead to hers and helped Carla off the counter to resume making his plate. Carla could count on Chrissey to bust her in front of everyone. It had been that way since the day they crossed the threshold of eighteen, their mouths poured just about anything out of it as long as their parents weren't too offended.

Carla didn't have a traditional family and she wasn't raised in a traditional household. Carlos and Eileen taught their children about God, to have the fear of God and to reverence God as the head of their lives. But, they didn't beat them over the head with the bible because no matter how many times a person attended service, prayed and read their Bible; every soul had to travel its own path. Carla was aware that her father could feel the attraction between Joshua and her and if he saw it, so did everyone else. Growing up in a God fearing home and being the daughter of a pastor ensured that the gifts and talents that the parents possessed normally resided on the children; more spiritual than natural.

Carla was certain that her gift of discernment picked up on what Joshua didn't and wouldn't say, especially regarding the reasoning for him not smiling much. His posture didn't say that he was dealing with some personal demons, but his eyes did. They spoke volumes and her holy ghost confirmed it. Being a Pastor's kid had advantages and disadvantages, but being able to pick up and feel the mood and motives of the people around you was definitely an advantage.

Before Carla could get through the kitchen doors to address her youngest sister, Joshua called out. "CeCe, is what they say about PK's true?"

"PK's huh?" It was interesting to know that he had some knowledge and terminology of church.

"Yes, Preacher Kids!" He reiterated.

"And what exactly do they say about us?" Carla stood at the doorway grinning and crossing her arms over her chest. She knew what he was about to say, but since his humor was present; missing out on this opportunity to explore it was not an option.

He could tell she was toiling with him, but he wanted to know the truth, his religious background was a little different and not as extensive as hers. "That y'all are some of the freakiest people that God has placed on this planet!!"

Walking in his direction, Carla stood in front of him, pressed her body completely against his and cradled the back of his head. Rising on her tippy toes; she placed her right hand on his zipper and stimulated the desire that had returned, extracting a moan deep down in his throat as she added more pressure. "If you keep fucking with me Sug, I promise for all the tea in China that I'm going to show you just how freaky I can be!" Letting him go, Carla walked out of the kitchen to pack her things.

At that moment it was best for both of them because Joshua was throwing off her concentration and Carla had a house full of guests that she considered dismissing and escorting to the door. She heard the lines "Get the steppin" from the show Martin running through her mind when he held the door open to throw Cole, Tommy and Pam out.

Walking into the living room, "Sorry y'all, come on Mommy, Morgan, Chrissey and Ebony!" Carla rounded them. When they were upstairs in her bedroom, Chrissey didn't waste any time, "If Ebony hadn't told me to mind my own business, I was definitely coming in to cock block."

"There's nothing to cock block." Carla was trying not to blush, but lying wasn't her forte and she couldn't really keep a straight face when joking around.

"You're lying, the attraction is definitely there." Ebony interrupted from inside of Carla's closet.

"Hello, I'm technically still married!" Carla tried to state calmly.

"Hello, you should have filed for divorce already, what are you waiting on?" Morgan added her two cents while taping up one of the boxes she had filled quickly.

Carla couldn't help but laugh, "He's as old as Daddy and old men have worms!"

"The hell they do!" Eileen blurted, she was sure she had heard enough.

"Mommy!" All four girls gasped and chorused, "Not your old man of course!"

"Okay, next subject!" Carla had to get control of the conversation because she didn't know enough about Joshua to declare that he was worthy of her or her time. Although, their current situation forced them to share the same space for the next five hours or so while traveling to Chicago.

CHAPTER 6

After an hour passed of continuous packing, Carla took a break to check on the men. The scene was quite interesting, Joshua fit right in there with the other three as they sat in front of the television watching a random movie on HBO. She quietly tipped-toed back upstairs to gather the remaining items that would make her hotel suite her home for the next three months.

An hour later the sporty Jeep was packed to capacity, luckily it was only Joshua and Carla traveling. With a five hour drive ahead they were expected to arrive in Chicago by 8pm EST/ 7pm CST. As the tires hit the tar on the freeway, Joshua turned on soft R&B that filled the car with the lyrical persuasions of Erykah Badu, Lauryn Hill, KC & JoJo, Tank, Genuine, Keith Sweat and various artists that fell into that genre of musicians.

"So are you going to talk to me or just drown me out with the music?" Carla cut into his thoughts.

"You think I'm drowning you out?" Joshua looked over and seen her raised eyebrow. "What do you want to talk about?"

"It doesn't matter, I just like to listen to you talk!" Carla admitted.

"Is that right?"

"It is."

"I want you to tell me about your husband!" Joshua disclosed.

"No." She stiffened, *what the hell was wrong with this guy?* "That subject is not up for discussion!"

He heard the finality in her voice and he knew that it had to be a touchy subject, so he would let it pass. "Promise to tell me when you feel comfortable?"

After a long deliberate pause with her head facing towards the window. "Sure."

"That's not the same things as 'I Promise'."

"I didn't promise, but I didn't say 'No' either!" No one understood that at one point, Carla loved the ground that her husband walked on. She could sense when things were right and when they were wrong. And it had taken years to love him, but not be in love with him and she wasn't willing to let anyone make her relive her past and reopen old scars.

Deciding to change the mood of the conversation, Joshua slowed the jeep down to reach his right hand towards Carla's face and forced her to look at him. That's when he saw it, she had shut down and he knew the look all too well because it mirrored the look in his eyes. "I think you have a lovely family." Was his comment instead of what he really wanted to say!

Smiling, "I think they were taken by you as well." She stroked his arm that was still firmly planted under her chin.

"I believe that no one should go through life without their parents, no matter how old you are it's nice to still have them around."

"How long ago did you lose your parents?" Feeling sorrow radiate off of him and then vanish.

"What makes you think that I lost my parents?"

"I can sense it!" Carla figured that he needed more of an explanation when he gave her the 'I don't buy it' face.

"It's a trick I learned and if I tell you, then I'll have to kill you."

Reflecting back on the conversation they had in her office when Joshua used the answer on her. He chortled, "Umm." Releasing out air from the pit of his stomach where he kept things buried. "Eight years ago with my mother and father, twelve years ago for my grandfather. My mother passed away around Thanksgiving and my father after Christmas. So the holidays aren't much of a joyous occasion and I don't bother to celebrate them."

In a quiet voice Carla murmured, "I'm Sorry." She didn't know of anything else to say because she couldn't begin to fathom what life would be like without her parents.

"Don't be, such is life!"

"That's a terrible philosophy!"

"Is that right?"

"That's correct, you need another coping mechanism. Tell me about your children!"

"You want me to share, but you don't want too?"

Shifting in her seat, "I just need some more time that's all; I never said that I wouldn't share."

Turning his head back to the road, "I have two sons and two daughters!"

"How old are they? Since they're older than me!"

Carla glanced at Joshua because he didn't respond, but he was beaming that she recalled his comment. "Yes, I remember your rude ass comment, so how old are they?"

"Jaden and Jayla are thirty years old, Jasmine is twenty-five and Jonathan is twenty."

"So you have a set of twins?"

"Yes, I had them at fifteen years old."

"Is that right?"

"Are you mocking me?"

"No sir."

"Earlier I was Suga then Daddy, now I'm Sir?"

"I think I like Sug!" Carla acknowledged.

"Why?"

"I don't know, it just sticks."

"Is that right?"

"Ha. Yes that's right!" Carla was lying. She didn't want to call him bay, baby, honey or any of the above because those were names that she had called her husband and in no way did she want that kind of connection with this man.

"Well I don't like abbreviations, I'm an old head and we spell our words out."

"Well I think you will live." Carla replied, trying to get use to his candor. I mean, she was direct and spoke her mind, but sometimes Joshua composed sentences that made you imagine someone sharpening iron.

Joshua started to exit the freeway and looked over and said, "We've been driving about two hours, are you hungry or need to use the bathroom?"

"Both, we ate breakfast almost six hours ago." Carla counted.

"Okay, we can eat anything except Wendy's, I worked there growing up and it's not one of my favorite meals."

"We can go to McDonald's so that you can get your fish sandwich, but for the record, I love Wendy's!"

After filling their stomachs and emptying their bladders, they returned to the highway making the five hour trip in four and a half hours. Pulling into the Four Seasons Hotel of Chicago, Carla started to feel some kind of way, almost home sick. When Joshua exited the car, she couldn't make her feet move so she sat there with the door open.

"CeCe what's the matter?" Joshua asked.

"I'm feeling home sick." Carla replied after a slight pause.

"Is that right?" He whispered to show his sincerity.

"Don't make fun of me Sug, I'm serious."

He lowered his head into the passenger side and said, "I can tell." Grabbing her hand and ducking out of the car, he gathered her into his embrace. Backing her body onto the exterior of the 2012 Jeep Cherokee, Joshua bent forward and gave her three brief, small kisses on the lips. "Your father told me to look after you and that's exactly what I intend to do, everything's going to be fine."

"I promise to God from Heaven to Earth that there is something seriously wrong with the male species, the shit you and Jeff were on, rubbed off on my Daddy."

"No, your father understands that I am a father as well with daughters and I'm not going to let anything happen to you. I told you that you're not here alone and you have me."

"I do not need a temporary daddy while I'm here."

Joshua stepped back.

O shit did I do it again? Her conscious screamed. *What I don't need is him transforming on me, considering that I really need him right now.* Carla thought to herself!

"Did I say anything about being your daddy? No." Joshua answered the question before she could. "But, I do plan to be daddy alright; I'm going to show you a whole new definition of the word. It will be a slight reminder to help you keep your mouth in check and your stank ass attitude under control."

Carla started grinning, "I'm sorry, I don't want to fall out with you right now. I need you to hang out with me for a while so I can warm up to this place."

Joshua grabbed her hand and pulled her towards the hotel doors to check in before bringing the luggage.

Approximately thirty minutes later, Joshua was ordering room service, while Carla made herself at home, placing all of her items in their perspective places. The dinner consisted of; chicken, rice, salad, bread, veggies and dessert which added to the exhaustion that had descended upon Carla's eyelids and weighed heavily on her shoulders.

Looking over at Carla, he watched her yawn. "You sleepy CeCe?"

"Yes, I'm sorry!" Carla tried to cover her mouth.

"Don't apologize, it's alright, I'm going to get ready and go!" Joshua put on his jacket.

"How far do you stay from here?"

"About twenty minutes, not too far."

"Oh okay, do you want me to drive you?"

"No, I'll call a cab."

"Are you sure?" Carla asked while trying to mask another yawn by covering her mouth.

"Yes Baby, get some rest." Bending onto the bed to kiss her, Carla pulled back and he paused, "What's the matter?"

"I never asked you if you had a girlfriend, significant other or someone you're currently seeing or sleeping with!"

"Don't you think you should have asked me that earlier?" He replied as he tucked his bottom lip under the top.

"That's not funny, but you're right, I should have and I didn't, but I'm asking now."

Joshua sat down on the bed and Carla moved over with her legs tucked underneath her butt. "I was seeing someone, but it was mainly physical. There were some things we didn't see eye to eye on."

"How long ago did the relationship end?"

"Seven months ago, she moved back to Pittsburgh, Pennsylvania."

Feeling a little more at ease, Carla laid her head on his shoulder. "Is that where you're initially from?"

"No I'm initially from here in Chicago, but I grew up in Pennsylvania." He kissed the top of her head. "I don't know what it is about you, but we click."

With her eyes closed and her consciousness losing a battle to stay awake, Carla yawned again. "Do you believe in monogamy?"

"In my old age I do, I only sleep with one woman at time."

"What does that mean?"

But, before Joshua could explain, Carla was silently snoring.

When Carla woke again it was 2:20am the next morning and her phone was vibrating on the dresser. She was laid on a sleeping and fully clothed Joshua; Carla couldn't remember when she fell asleep or why he stayed. Crossing the room to answer her cell, it dawned on her that she never called her family to let them know that she made it to Chicago safely.

"Hi Daddy!" Carla breathed into the phone.

"I'm assuming you lost all evidence of home-training while driving in the car with that old man for five hours. You forgot to call the most important man in your life to let him know that you had arrived safely."

Giggling. "Nobody, but you. I'm sorry Daddy, I was so exhausted that I fell asleep, but I made it."

"Good, well get some rest and call me later to let me know how your first day goes."

"Promise."

"Night Night Honey."

"Night Night Daddy!"

Ending the call and staring at the body laying in her bed, Carla was unsure if she should wake him or allow him to sleep. She didn't have a training class until Friday, but she was required to go in and meet with the managers and staff tomorrow. Since Joshua didn't have anything to change into for work, she figured that she should at least give him the option to be driven home.

Shaking him lightly, "Sug, wake up, we fell asleep!" Joshua didn't stir at all, so Carla tried again. "Honey you have to get up, we have to work in the morning and you don't have any clothes!"

Joshua shifted his body enough to say, "We can stop by my house in the morning, I'll go in late. What time is it?"

"It's almost 3am." Realizing that he had no interest in leaving tonight, Carla climbed back out of the bed and into the shower. Twenty minutes later, Carla exited the bathroom startled by Joshua who was sitting upright on the bed. She noticed the change in his comfort level and that stopped her in the midst of her tracks. "What's the matter?"

With sleep still in his eyes, he replied. "It's too warm in here."

"Let me turn the air on because if you get naked, then your ass will be on the couch." Carla expressed, partially joking.

Rising off of the bed in Carla's direction, he looked her in her eyes. "You scared?"

"Of what?" She jerked her head.

"Of you accidentally slipping onto my penis if I get naked!" Joshua joked.

Without warning, Carla's smile turned into laughter, "What is wrong with you?"

"Whatever, I know the dick good!" Joshua said confidently.

"Your opinion of how good your sex is, doesn't count!"

"Then I'll let you be the judge of that!"

Carla was in disbelief that she was having this conversation with him. "Do you have conversations like these on a regular basis?"

"Not at all, it's rare that I allow people to get close enough to even see me joke or smile! I have realized that you can't trust everybody, so it's better to be cutoff and unattached than hurt and disappointed."

"So you have massive trust issues?"

"Yes and I'm fine with that." Joshua admitted.

Carla saw the finality in his tone and decided to change his demeanor by closing the distance between them. "If I was scared, there's no way I would have fallen asleep no matter how tired I was." Walking around him to the drawer of clothes, "You can wear a pair of my shorts if you want to take a shower."

Joshua gave her a death stare so she continued as if she didn't see it. "My ass is wider than yours so they should hang nicely."

Reaching his hand out for the shorts, Joshua headed for the bathroom, but by the time he returned Carla was sleep again. He climbed in the bed and moved his hands under the covers trying to pull her into his arms. For reasons known and unknown he was drawn to her.

The morning came in a flash, they were awake by 7am. Carla got dressed and Joshua dressed in the clothes from the day before. He was awestruck by the sight of Carla, but he didn't have to say it because the admiration was in his gaze. She blew him a kiss once she caught the look and he grabbed her by the arm. "Don't start something you can't finish! Where are your keys?"

Handing over her keys, Carla grabbed the necessities to get her through the day and they exited the room as he held the door open for her to walk out. The sway in her stride gave Joshua a thorough view of what he could look forward too, but for now he was content with looking without touching!"

CHAPTER 7

*C*arla took a seat once they entered his house; he had nice taste for a bachelor. There was a living room and dinner room decorum that complimented the blinds and praised the center pieces and picture-frames that decorated the space. She patiently waited thirty minutes while Joshua hopped back in the shower and dressed in the back of the condo. Entering the living room, Joshua said, "I ordered us some breakfast from a small diner along the way, I don't want you hungry on your first day in the office." Acknowledging her smile, "We can do this one or two ways, you can ride with me to work or you can follow behind me."

Looking down at her hands to focus, Carla didn't want him to see the indecision in her eyes. Her equilibrium was in jeopardy because of the way he smelled and how good he looked in his slacks, shirt and vest. Her kitty cat definitely escalated from zero to ten so all she could say was, "I'll follow behind you because I believe I have monopolized enough of your time, don't you?"

"Huh?" Joshua was completely confused until realization dawned on him. "You suffer from passive-aggressive along with your bi-polar stank ass attitude disorder!"

"Excuse me?" Carla rose off of the couch.

"It's a clinical term, look it up!"

"I guess you have a psychology degree to accompany your degree in being an asshole! With your highly contagious case of bi-polar your damn self!"

"No, but I do have a bullshit meter." Joshua attacked.

"How in the fuck, am I bullshitting?" Carla's temper was almost through the roof, but Joshua wasn't backing down. *He was just as upset, but what could be his reasoning?* She pondered. "What month is your birthday in?" Carla unconsciously switched the topic.

"What?" Joshua roared.

"What month is your birthday in?" Carla repeated.

"What does that have to do with anything?"

"Just answer the question please!"

"March!" Joshua obliged.

"Are you a Pisces or an Aries?" Carla's brain was scrambling.

"Aries!" Joshua confirmed.

As if a light had switched on inside of Carla's brain, "That's what the fuck is wrong with you!" she directed the statement more to herself than Joshua.

"For a Pastor's daughter, you sure don't carry yourself in a saved, sanctified manor! Your mouth is filthy." Joshua stated.

More than offended at this point, Carla squared her shoulders. "You're one prayer away from a first class seat in hell yourself and to be honest you don't have to say shit to me. Nor do you have to engage in conversation with me if my mouth is too foul for you. But, please understand that I am human just like everyone else, including your issued ass."

Carla continued to attack him. "I have been cursing since the 3rd grade and it's called a strong hold, it's something that keeps you bound. Just like your trust issues, your bi-polar tendencies and the fact that you cut yourself off from people to cover your own ass. You are just as unstable as me or maybe worse because you pull me in just to turn me away and you definitely can kiss my ass with your judgmental bias that you seem to be over there passing."

They stood in the middle of Joshua's living room, his jaw was twitching and his chest was heaving in such a way that she could tell he was beyond pissed.

"Grab your things; I need to get to work!" Joshua insisted.

Knowing that she crossed the line, but not really caring a whole bunch at this point. Carla was beyond frustrated, she had trust issues just like he did, but she battled them differently. She hadn't opened herself up to anyone since her husband and if she could help it then she never would. Carla watched as Joshua quietly grabbed his work badge, laptop bag, keys, cell phone and moved towards the door. She was trying to protect herself from him because he was quickly rattling the chains she had securing around her heart.

Settling into the driver seat of her car, Carla began ranting. "Maybe I misbehaved and went too far, but I had no choice but to put some space in between us. What kind of nicca spends the night with a chick that he doesn't know, orders her breakfast and rides to work together? This isn't a got damn relationship." She was screaming out loud. "But, maybe I'm over thinking this; maybe he was just trying to be nice. That's what's wrong with women we misconstrue actions and information." She heard her subconscious rear its head and say, *"Not everyone that's nice to you, wants to be with you."*

When they walked into the building at 9am, Joshua informed Security that Carla needed to take a picture for her I.D.Badge. He waited quietly while the procedure was completed and then showed her to her desk. Joshua handed Carla the breakfast, while giving her the itinerary for the day and directing her to the department lead that worked under him. His mannerism was professional and closed off; once Carla finished her breakfast she went in search of the team lead.

Carla didn't comprehend what prompted the events at Joshua's house, walking in the direction of the team lead, she whispered. "This is exactly why I can't afford to deal with him because he throws me off my square. Why would he dump me off on his team lead when I was assigned to him?"

"Are you talking to yourself?" The lady stepped in Carla's path.

Startled by the intrusion of her personal thoughts, "Something like that." Carla couldn't help, but smile because she wanted to lie, but couldn't.

"Well, it happens to the best of us, I do believe that you're looking for me! My name is Taylor Wixom."

"Indeed I am, how are you? I'm Carla Williams."

"Nice to meet you Carla, I'm good, how is your first day thus far?"

"I actually just got here, but Joshua gave me an itinerary and instructed me to meet up with you!" Carla responded politely, but her initial explanation would have been what an asshole Joshua was and how much this morning had sucked ass. But, she was working on being a lady and that response would have been inappropriate.

"Yes the itinerary, we can go over it and I will show you around and help you get familiar with everything and everyone. You also have a meeting this afternoon with Joshua and the managers within this location."

"Perfect, sounds good to me!"

Smiling, Taylor could tell she was going to like Carla, "Follow me and we'll get started."

For the next two hours, Carla was on the move; meeting, greeting, smiling, and laughing with everyone that Taylor ran into. The atmosphere was very professional, yet warm and friendly and Carla could get use to being there for the next two to three months.

Around 1pm, Taylor advised that they were breaking for lunch and would reconvene around 2pm to gather their thoughts before the manager's meeting. Walking back to her desk, Carla's mind returned back to Joshua, it had been hours since she had spotted him. A huge part of her wanted to go in search of him, but that would make her vulnerable so she would wait and see if he would seek her out first.

Grabbing her purse and badge, Carla exited the building to find the nearest restaurant for lunch. 2pm came and went without any hiccups; Joshua attended the management meeting, but never looked in her direction and only said her name to reference his visit to Michigan. The meeting adjourned with Carla being excused for the remainder of the day with an update that her first training class would be Monday instead of Friday. Walking back to her desk, she waited ten minutes, hoping that Joshua would come and say something to her, but he never showed.

Carla walked into the hotel and headed towards her room. She was hoping and praying that Joshua's attitude wouldn't last long because he was the only person that she knew in the state. Unconsciously, she trusted that if Joshua would do anything, he wouldn't abandon her. Carla recognized that her disposition needed some adjusting, but she had been working on not being so defensive. He just happened to ruffle her feathers more than the other individuals that she engaged with.

Taking off her clothes, settling into her suite and calling her father as promised led to calls with her best friend and sister. The communication helped with some of the anxiety that Carla was beginning to feel. For about sixty seconds she even considered calling her husband because even though he had taken her to hell and back, she knew that he would love her forever. Sleep consumed Carla and the tension and sadness of possibly being all alone for the remainder of this business trip drifted.

CHAPTER 8

August 17, 2012

Strolling into the doors of Humility Bank of Chicago Friday morning, Carla had a new attitude; it was ok if Joshua no longer wanted to be bothered. She made a conscious decision that a return trip home to Michigan every other weekend to be with her family was the solution. And on the alternate weekends she would take the time to sightsee and indulge in the state's extracurricular activities that it offered. Badging into the system and pulling Joshua's watch out of her purse that he left on her night stand, Carla headed towards his desk. Noticing that he was absent from his chair, she left it on his keyboard. She was content with the fact if he wanted to thank her for it, he knew where to find her.

For the rest of the morning, Carla went to the training room that she was assigned and began setting everything in place while revising slides according to the flow of the environment. The energy from the people was pleasant in Chicago, so it would be a pleasure to introduce and transition them over to Serenity's way of business. By the time lunchtime came, Carla was starving. Clutching her belongings to depart the building she ran into Joshua, but not stopping to address him. He didn't speak until they were outside of the doors. "Hey Carla, did you get my email?"

Carla slowed her pace, but didn't completely stop. "No, I haven't been at my desk all morning."

"I was just thanking you for my watch."

"No problem, you're welcome! Have a good lunch."

Before Joshua could squeeze in another sentence, Carla picked up her pace. She didn't have time to play games with him and she couldn't afford to be caught up in his web. He was charming, smooth and a joy to be around, but she refused to fall prey without the certainty that he would ultimately feel the same.

Once lunch was over, Carla went back to her training room to make sure that everything was all set and ready for Monday. She had printed booklets of the guidelines, procedures, policy's and the first week of training manuals. The excitement of why she came to Chicago had returned when the knock at the door startled her.

Turning her attention to the already opened door, Carla saw Taylor standing. "Hey can I come in?" Taylor asked.

"Of course you can, how are you Taylor?"

"It's been a pretty easy day, I came down to invite you to our Friday outing that we have after work!"

"Wow, thank you, where do you guys normally go?" Carla smiled.

"Just around the corner to the local bar today, but we indulge in bowling, pool, restaurants, etc!"

Not really feeling like herself nor in the mood to be surrounded by a bunch of people, Carla declined the offer. "How about I make it my business to show up next Friday, I'm still trying to get settled."

"Of course, well just know that the invitation is open!"

"Thank you Taylor, I appreciate it!" It was nice for Carla to know that they wanted her to truly be a part of the team. Even if she wasn't much of a drinker and she had never smoked anything in her life. Besides her cursing habit, she didn't really have any other habits that she struggled with.

Returning to an empty hotel with no one to talk too, she did the next best thing, she went in search of something to eat. Carla agreed to spend her weekend getting into her role as the trainer while pulling her emotions under control. Tonight would consist of dinner and a movie. Saturday she would do a little research on a hair shop for a press and curl, followed by a pedicure and a fill-in for her over lay.

For Sunday, Carla considered church hunting. She had never been one to church hop or visit random churches because she was raised that's how spirits were transferred. When you went from church to church and allowed various people to speak and minister over your soul, it left you open and uncovered. But, she needed to hear the Word and sit under someone's teaching to keep herself encouraged

Breaking into her thoughts, her cell phone started spitting the lyrics of Rick Ross's *Money Makes Me Cum* and she immediately knew who was calling. Answering the phone with the swipe of her fingers, "Hi Pooty!"

"Hi Boo, what you doing?" Chrissey asked.

"Nothing what's up with you Chrissey?"

"Girl, I called to tell you about this bullshit!"

"What happened?" Carla automatically geared into attack mode. She was a protector by nature and although all of her sisters were grown, she would go to war for them at any cost.

"Man, I shitted on myself!" Chrissey elaborated.

Carla was completely startled by the turn of the conversation. "Huh?"

"You heard me. I went and got my colon cleansed. I tried to warn the lady before she stuck that hose up my ass that I was shitter and she didn't believe me."

Laughing uncontrollably at the image of Chrissey losing her bowls. "Wait, Wait, Wait, so you shitted on yourself during the colon cleansing process?"

"Girl, I shitted during and after the cleansing process. I thought I was finished until I started driving home and felt the urge again, but by the time I made it to Burger King I had messed up the seats in my truck."

Chrissey was more prideful than any person Carla knew and she kept it real, but Carla knew that Chrissey was more pissed off than she led on about the incident. "So how did you go in the house without anyone seeing you?"

"I didn't go home; I stopped over Tasha's house to change first. There was no way I was going to enter my building and run the risk of bumping into a fine hunk of a man while smelling like a hospital patient!"

Laughing at the retardation that emitted off of Chrissey and the way her brain process was set up. Carla was thankful for the delightful distraction that her sister temporarily provided her. At that moment, she missed being home more than anything.

By the time Sunday rolled around, Carla felt a little more at home, she vetoed the idea of going to look for a church. Her mind was more concerned with the fact that Joshua hadn't said one word to her all weekend. Had the argument been that deep to make him retreat? Or, was it that he returned home and she was just of mere convenience while they were in Michigan?

Pulling out her tablet, Carla wanted to research the characteristics of an Aries to gain some clarity. Settling onto the Google website, the information only confirmed what Carla had dreaded. A relationship with Joshua would be difficult and harmony would be scarce, an Aries man and a Capricorn woman were not compatible. People like Joshua were confrontational, arrogant, stubborn and impulsive excitement seekers that never stayed in one place too long.

Positioning back on the bed, Carla closed her eyes, she couldn't ponder on the issue, but she would treat him the same way he treated her.

Monday Morning—Aug. 20, 2012

Preparing for work, Carla unwrapped her hair and slipped on some sexy wedge heels to compliment her skirt suit that stopped mid thigh with a jacket that was pleated with ruffles. She even went as far as to slide her 3.5 Karat wedding ring on that her husband had purchased for her six years prior.

Walking into Humility's building doors, she was unstoppable. She decided to stop at her desk and lock her things away in her drawers because everything she needed had been prepped Friday and was ready to go. Logging into the systems, Carla put in her time and checked the communicator that allowed her to chat with anyone that worked within the company. She briefly skimmed her emails and then logged out to head down to the training room.

When Carla got to the end of the aisle she ran into Taylor, "Oh, well don't you look pretty?" Taylor complimented.

"Thank you Taylor, I couldn't come in here on my first day of training, looking like who shot John and forgot to kill him!"

Laughing immediately, Taylor recognized the line from Love and Basketball. "I do believe I am going to enjoy you being here!"

"I hope I can say the same, your boss seems to be giving me the cold shoulder. So that leaves me with no one to talk to, eat lunch with, sightsee or any of the above!"

"Girl Boom, Joshua is a chameleon, he goes in and out. But, don't worry about any of those other things, we will exchange numbers and since I don't have a man or children, I'm free!"

Carla smiled at the thought that she might be able to find a friend in Taylor. "Perfect, well I'll see you in class shortly."

"Okay, I'll be there in a minute." Taylor assured.

In the back of her mind, it made Carla feel a little better that Joshua was uptight by nature and not just because her mouth was a tad bit disrespectful.

Prancing to her room, Carla slowed her steps when she realized that her door was already open and the lights were on. Entering the threshold once she realized who her first trainee was that happened to arrive before class.

"Looking for something?" Carla asked sweetly.

"No, I was looking for someone!" Joshua smiled when he turned around to face her. He didn't want to admit it, but he had missed her. Maybe he was being a little hard on her considering they were two adults.

"Did you find them or are you still searching?" Carla probed further.

Walking passed her to close the door for them to have a few moments alone before the class joined. "I just wanted to talk to you for a minute."

"Sure, what's up?"

Walking and standing directly in front of Carla, "I just wanted to make sure you were good."

"That's interesting because I believe I spent this weekend alone in my hotel room!"

"I think we both needed some time to cool off!" Joshua tried to explain.

"Cool off? The incident happened almost five days ago. You knew I wouldn't know anyone, were you trying to teach me some kind of lesson?" When he didn't respond, Carla knew she had the answer. "This isn't a game and I am not a child. So the joke is on you because I'm good from here on out!" Carla knew that she didn't mean most of what she said, but she was through dealing with his shitty behavior.

Clenching his fist, trying to tame his temper, Joshua was a man who prided himself on self control. "Whatever Carla, but understand that it's your mouth and I am not going to deal with it!"

"Okay, then don't!"

Walking away without responding, Joshua knew that the respect on his end was going to depreciate if he opened his mouth. It had taken him years and much practice to learn how to control his anger and temperament. He used to be a hot head just like Carla without the estrogen, so he would resort back to the silent treatment.

Ten minutes later the class began to file in, totaling a co-ed number of twenty-five people. At 8:30am everyone was seated in a chair with pens, pads and their eyes molded to Carla.

Feeling a need to say something, Carla began with introductions. "Hello, on your desk you will find a folded, cardboard name slot, just like in school." She smiled at the few snickers around the room. "Until I am able to memorize your names, please fill them out and stand it up or lay it down in a way that I can see the name." Concluding her sentence, Joshua joined the class, taking a seat in the back.

"I would like for everyone to go around the room and tell me your name and something about yourself, I'll go first. My name is Carla Williams, I am the Head Trainer at the new corporate office in Michigan and I have been training for the last five years with Serenity Bank. I obtained my Bachelors Degree from Michigan State University in Training and Development and my Master's Degree from Oakland University in Communications."

Yelling out from the back of the room, a gentleman with a name tag that read DARIUS asked. "Are you married with children?" Darius grinned a chest cat smile, while obtaining a chorus of harmonious ruckus. It confirmed that the men were more interested in the question than the women.

Blushing and bowing her head for a moment to see how she wanted to respond. "I am married, but separated, with no children."

"Then why are you still wearing his ring?" Darius couldn't help but probe.

"Technically it's my ring and because I am in a state all by myself, I felt like these girls were the only friends I had to keep me company!" Wriggling her fingers, Carla couldn't think of a better friend than a 3.5 Karat diamond ring.

"Now, that Darius has completely exploited my business, he can be the first one to make introductions!" Carla grasped a light-hearted laugh from the class and the introductions began.

At 12 pm, class was dismissed for a one hour lunch and everyone agreed to hold the breaks until the second half of class. Everything seemed to be floating smoothly. Joshua was proud that Carla could handle herself because he had prepared himself for the men who would admire her shapely body and sweet perfume just as he had. If things would have worked out differently he would have loved to sample just how sweet she was on top of her training desk. Shaking his head to gain control and eliminate the urge that came unexpectedly from being around her.

Before Joshua could ask her to join him for lunch, Taylor intervened. "Would you like to eat lunch with me Carla?"

Lifting her head to Taylor's request and also seeing Joshua approaching as well, "Sure!" Turning her body slightly, "Was there something you needed Joshua?"

Joshua stammered when he realized that Carla didn't miss that he was initially going to say something to her. "Nothing that I can't mention later."

Leaving the classroom and heading into the cafeteria for lunch Carla began to relax. She wasn't the kind of person who put herself in positions for people to reject her, regardless of the relationship. Once she confirmed that the people who were surrounded around her were genuine, she could relax.

When Carla arrived back from lunch, she resumed with training. Everyone took notes, asked questions, received clarity and seemed to grasp the concepts of how Serenity banked in the loan; mortgage and credit card industry.

Later on that evening, Carla heard a knock at the door and she thought Joshua had finally come to his senses. But, when she swung the door open, her husband stood in the doorway.

Dre was the first to speak. "Hey Honey, I'm home!"

Carla stepped aside to let Dre into the suite with her facial features expressing mixed emotions of shock and surprise. She asked, "What are you doing here? How did you know where to find me?"

Dre hugged Carla and explained, "I spoke with your mother. I'm out here for a few days and I offered to come and check on you."

Carla could count on Eileen to rat her out. Dre had been a son to her in every sense of the word. Pulling herself back to the present, Carla responded. "Of course my mother would tell you!"

Dre released Carla from his snug hold and used his hand to tilt her chin, "She's our mother, Honey."

Unable to hold her composure, Carla laughed. "Please tell me that you're seeking help because you're getting crazier each time I see you."

"Technically you're still my wife so we're all still family." Dre assured her.

Carla took a seat on her bed and shook her head. *This was going to be a long night*, she mused quietly.

"What can I do for you Honey?" Carla decided to entertain her husband. It wasn't as if she had anything else to do tonight.

Dre smiled at Carla, showing all thirty two teeth. "Actually, I'd like for you to accompany me to dinner this evening!"

"Okay, do I need to change?"

"No, you're fine as always!" Dre couldn't help, but admire.

Carla smiled at him, Dre was always as smooth as a can of paint, but she was immune to his manipulation.

Forty-five minutes later, Dre and Carla arrived at Lawry's Prime Rib and Steakhouse. After the formation of ordering appetizers and entrées, Dre opened the arena for conversation.

"CeCe, I missed you, you've been too busy for me lately."

"I've been training and getting accustomed to how they do things here." Carla said as she arranged her silverware.

"Are you seeing anyone?" Dre questioned.

Carla knew the bullshit was coming, she was waiting on it. "No, I'm not, are you?"

"I'm trying to see you CeCe. I love you, you're my wife and that's never going to change."

"Yeah, I know Dre!" Carla smirked, trying to cover up her disgust.

Carla tried to change the conversation to general conversation topics that ranged from families, jobs to new endeavors and business ideas.

When Dre walked Carla back to her door, he leaned her against the wall in an attempt to kiss her. But, Carla turned her head and he stepped back.

Carla stared at his unraveling composure. "You're always trying to get fresh with me!"

"And you're always refuting my advances." He disputed.

"Because I don't know where your lips have been, let alone your penis." She spat.

Dre backed Carla into the wall, "But, I know where they want to be."

Carla didn't mean to, but she spit in Dre's face when the laughter sprang from her throat. She tried to wipe the spit away, but Dre moved out of her reach.

"Take your spitting, silly ass in your room; I have to get back on the road." Dre urged.

Carla reached for him again, "I'm sorry love, we'll talk sometime next week." She pushed the key into the slot and waited for the light to turn green. Kissing Dre's cheek, she thanked him for the food and wished him a goodnight.

Unwinding across her bed, Carla thought of Dre's appearance and couldn't help, but wish that she had spent the evening with Joshua instead.

Two Weeks Later—Aug. 31, 2012

Before Carla knew it, the two week class was complete and it was time for the class to take their assessment. She had to train six classes at approximately two weeks a piece and then she would remain in the office for an additional two weeks for questions and concerns if management saw fit.

The routine that Carla had enforced every Friday in training allowed her to provide cupcakes, candy, chips and other light snacks for ending the week on a good note. The treats helped keep everyone engaged, along with the miniature size candies for class discussions and participation. It was an inexpensive price to pay for the ultimate goal of no one crashing her course.

At the end of class, Taylor reminded Carla that she promised to attend the next function from the previous two weeks when she opted out. Carla never went back on her word, but she was more than discouraged. Another week had passed and Joshua hadn't said one word or made any additional advances. He had escalated the word 'ignore' to a new level and she was angry, hurt, disappointed, hostile and sad all at the same time.

"You can follow me to the bowling alley for tonight's event Carla." Taylor said as she walked over to Carla's desk as she packed to leave.

"Umm, sure!" Giving Taylor a laugh. It seemed as if Taylor was determined to make Carla apart of the team and although she didn't mind, Carla really just wanted Joshua back. He had awaken the womanly part of her that she kept suppressed since her husband insisted on screwing every chick he had come in contact with. Thankfully, Dre was kind enough not to infect her with any sexually transmitted diseases, but she sure as shit wasn't going to wait around for him to do so.

Leaving the building and walking to her car, she caught Joshua's eye and he started gearing in her direction, "Are you coming out tonight?"

"Oh now you see me?" Carla snarled.

"You probably should tuck that attitude or its going to be a long night!" Joshua retorted.

"It's a long night every night! You made me think that you were going to be here with me during this transition. When in fact, all you did was abandon me at the first sign that I would put up a fight!"

"Because I fucking refuse to argue with you, life is too short and my life is too complicated to add anymore bullshit on top of it."

"Okay, so don't." Turning her back towards him and attempting to get in her truck because she was offended at his irrational rationale. Carla didn't want to complicate his life, but she didn't want to be considered as bullshit either.

Joshua stopped her from entering the car, "Now you're the one running at the first sign of trouble!"

"I'm not running, but I don't have time for you to be rude to me either. You can't justify this; you're old as hell. Are you telling me that we couldn't have talked it out? You would rather leave me in a hotel room, where I hibernate day in and day out? I don't know where to go and I don't have any one to go with!" Carla was panting with frustration.

Watching from across the parking lot sat the team in amusement as they witnessed the exchange between the two. It was Taylor who finally asked Carla, "Are you ready to head over?"

Stepping in front of Carla and speaking before she could, Joshua replied. "She can follow behind me, I got her Taylor!"

Lifting her eyebrow, but resolving not to intervene any further, "Okay, I'll see you guys there!"

Joshua turned back in Carla's direction and whispered, "If you surrender then I promise to be nice!" But Carla's eyes were so low that he thought they were closed until he saw the tear slide down her cheek. Joshua lifted her face to look at his, but Carla still didn't lift her lids. "Baby why are you crying?" Wiping a tear that fell and watching her in silence, hoping for a reply, but when Carla said nothing, he whispered again. "Baby why are you crying? Don't cry!" Carla didn't say a word, but more tears ran down her cheeks. Joshua was helpless and he didn't know what to do, maybe he had taken things too far.

Using his thumbs and wiping her tears, she placed both of her hands around his wrists when he bent over and kissed her lips. "I'm sorry CeCe, I went too far. I shouldn't have left you alone Babe." Making more tears flood her eyes while he kissed her again, "I'm sorry Baby." They forgot about the people lingering around them when he pulled her into his embrace and held Carla until he felt her body stop trembling.

When Carla let him go, he wiped the remaining moisture off of her face. Joshua silently admitted that she was pretty with or without makeup. At that moment, he made a mental note of the fact that even though Carla talked a good game, she was extremely sensitive.

"Spend the night with me?" he asked.

Speaking for the first time since the waterworks, Carla asked shocked, "Tonight?"

"Yes!"

"At your house?"

"Yes!" Joshua confirmed.

Carla paused to think if this was really a good idea, but it was evident that she missed his company and he seemed to have missed her. "Okay."

Kissing her lips again, "Let's go to the hotel first, you can grab some clothes and we will get in one car."

When they pulled into the hotel's parking lot, Carla ran inside the hotel while Joshua stayed in the car. She packed a bag with her hair products, pajamas, under garments and clothes for Saturday and Sunday, just in case. Pulling the handle of her car door to make sure it was locked and sliding into the passenger side of Joshua's 2011 GMC Yukon, Carla was finally at peace.

Joshua pulled out of the parking spot and pulled into Timber Lanes Bowling Alley. Once they entered the facility, Carla noticed that they were the last two people to join the crew and all eyes were on them. Steering towards the counter to pay for their bowling lane and shoes, Carla went into her purse and Joshua whispered. "When you're with me, you don't have to worry about anything, I have it."

Joshua reached into his wad of money and handed the man thirty dollars for the unlimited bowl and shoes. She couldn't help, but smile to herself, Joshua was such a gentleman when he wanted to be. Carla couldn't relax her guard just yet though, he was too wishy washy for her to get comfortable.

As soon as they found the others, Joshua immediately began mingling while Carla sat in a chair to put on her bowling shoes. Within seconds of her ass hitting the hard plastic Taylor joined her. "Umm, I'm not trying to meddle or anything, but it seems like you and Jay have been holding out."

Knowing that the assumptions would start coming full force, Carla had mentally prepared herself on the way over, but Joshua didn't seem the least bit phased by it. "Holding out on what?"

Cocking her neck to the side, Taylor gave Carla the 'don't play with me' glare.

Laughing at the non-verbal communication, Carla explained. "I don't know what you mean, we're not holding out on anything!"

"I mean that the chemistry is extremely high between you two and you're more bubblier than you've been since you got here!" Taylor continued to meddle.

"Is that right?"

"And now you're using Jay's favorite words!"

Carla giggled because she knew Taylor was right, Carla couldn't count the number of times Joshua would say 'Is that right' once he was set in his cynical mode. "Look, I like Jay, but there's not much to tell at this point, I'm still trying to get pass the mood swings!"

"After, he's a little more comfortable with you, the swinging should turn into rocking." Smiling as if she was letting Carla in on a little secret.

"How long have you two worked together?" Carla asked before realizing that she may have seemed a little territorial.

"It will be seven years in November. He can be a piece of work, but he's very intelligent and extremely wise."

"Yeah I can tell." Carla responded while tying up her shoes, but when she lifted her head Joshua was staring at her. Locking eyes, it was as if Joshua could reach into her soul and unlock every emotion that she commanded to remain dormant.

Walking towards her with their eyes still locked, Joshua bent down and asked, "Do you want something to drink or eat from the concession stand?"

"I'm okay for now."

"Will you let me know when you do?"

"Yes."

The next three hours went by with fun filled, light hearted, competitive, trash-talking, beer drinking, disco dancing fellowship. Heading to the car and saying goodnight to everyone, Joshua opened up the car door for Carla and then walked around to slide in beside her. Looking at her head rested on the seat, "You're sleepy."

"Yes, I am, do you want me to go home instead of your house?"

"Oh, there she is. I thought you had alleviated the passive aggressive Carla of her duties for tonight?" Joshua asked sarcastically.

"You're such an ass; I just wanted to give you an out if you needed one." Carla explained.

"Have I had a problem communicating anything to you since meeting you?"

"NO, definitely not." While rolling her eyes to make sure he picked up on her sarcasm.

"I promise you won't have to assume with me, all you have to do is ask." Joshua assured.

Grabbing his hands and threading them through hers, Carla lowered her eyelids to cover her inner most thoughts. She was well aware that he was still looking at her so she lifted her lids slowly so that he could see exactly what she meant when she opened her mouth. "Will you hold me tonight?"

Carla hated asking anyone for anything, but tonight she needed him to hold her. It had been two long weeks of pretending that she didn't care and that she didn't feel anything. But, when he wiped her tears and kissed her outside of Humility Bank, he stripped her of that. All Carla wanted to do was go home with him, shower, put on her pajamas, crawl into bed and let him wrap his arms around her.

Shocked at the request, he knew he couldn't deny her of that, he had missed her too. Pressing towards her, Joshua swiped her cheek and brushed his hand through her hair. "Of course Sug!"

Smiling at his choice term for an endearment, Carla bit her lower lip, inclined into him and for the first time since they had met, she initiated the kiss.

CHAPTER 9

*R*eaching the front of his home and climbing the steps of his porch, Joshua unlocked the door, grabbed Carla's bag and entered the house. Carla walked straight to the bathroom as if Joshua had previously given her a personal tour. When she went in search of him, she found him in his bedroom, stretched out on the bed with his forearm over his forehead. "I guess I'm not the only one that's sleepy!"

"I'll be okay once I take a shower!" Lifting his arm slightly. "Go ahead and go first and then I'll follow in behind you!"

"Okay!" Carla answered.

Fifteen minutes later Carla emerged from the bathroom to a light-snoring Joshua. She bent down to untie his shoes and slowly removed them from his feet along with his socks. Joshua sat up, "What you doing Mami'?"

"Nothing, I was trying to help you get a little bit more comfortable." Carla leaned back as Joshua rose off the bed to finish what she started.

"I appreciate it, let me get in the shower and put on a movie or something." Joshua walked passed Carla as she sat on the bed.

Twenty minutes later, Joshua exited the bathroom and entered the bedroom to find Carla still sitting in the same position. Noticing that they both had flannel pajama pants and t-shirts as their night wear. He swiped his hand over her nipples, grasping her attention with a sharp intake of air.

"You don't sleep in a bra or anything Babe?" He sat down on the bed beside her.

Looking Joshua in his eyes, she waited for him to invite her to invade his personal space. "Don't start something you're not willing to finish." Standing up Carla pushed him onto the bed while straddling his legs and placing her nicely shaped ass on his hardening penis. "Because I am more than ready!" All the while, gyrating her hips causing her butt to slide back and her center to press against his covered flesh.

Flipping her on her back, Joshua dipped his body into Carla, allowing her to feel his length. "Mami' I'm not a kid, don't tease me."

Carla trapped his waist with her legs to drive her point home. "Does it look like I'm teasing you?"

Even though every fiber of his being wanted to bury his well endowed instrument into her vessel, he needed to know more about her. He wanted to spend more time with her! As he inclined his body totally over hers, Joshua whispered close to ear. "I want to get to know more of you before I come after your body!"

Completely shocked at his revelation, Carla sat up, forcing him to move from in between her legs. "You're a mysterious man Mr. Williams. What is it that you would like to know?"

"I want you to tell me about your husband and your marriage!" He confirmed.

"And I want to know that you're not going to abandon me again while I'm in your care and your state." She countered.

"I'm not going to abandon you anymore." Joshua confirmed.

Falling back against the head board of the bed, "You promise?"

Pulling her onto his lap as he slid his back onto the head board, "Promise." And sealed it with a kiss.

Opening his legs further apart, Carla glided back off of Joshua's lap so that her butt was on the bed, but her legs were on each side of his body. "Hmmm, where do I begin? Wait, first can you tell me why it's so important for you to know?"

"Before I invest anymore of myself into you, I need to know where you and I are headed and if there is any chance of reconciliation between you two, if so, then I'll know my place."

Nodding her head at his confession and taking a deep breath, Carla exhaled. "I met Dre in middle school. He was cool, laid back and a real jokester. He's two weeks older than me so we got along pretty great. For years, we were really great friends and when it was time to go off to high school we went our separate ways, but stayed in touched."

"We never crossed the line of friendship until my senior year in high school." Carla paused before proceeding. "I attended prom with him at his school and he attended my prom as well. He was my first real boyfriend, my first love and when I was twenty-one years old, he asked me to marry him. In 2005, I married Andre Davis and in 2007 we separated, but by 2008 I filed for a legal separation."

"Why didn't you file for a divorce instead of legal separation?" Joshua posed.

"Because he fought me on the divorce, gave me a really hard time, wouldn't sign the paperwork, was crying at my door and following me to work. It became so much that I dropped off of the face of the earth for a while. I filed for a stress leave at work and I started seeing a shrink."

Watching her intently, Joshua began reading her body language. "What else happened, Sug?"

Resting her head against his shoulder, Carla started taking small short breaths to calm her heart-rate; she refused to have a panic attack over this. Joshua was asking her to relive this scene for scene. "To say that I loved him was an understatement; we breathed the same air and when things got rough and shit hit the fan, I was the ride or die chick. To this day, I know that he loves me, but I also know that people only change because they want to and because they are tired of their own bullshit. I'm not convinced that he will ever completely change."

Joshua placed his hand on the back of her head and turned her head slightly so that he could kiss her cheek. "Tell me what happened, Baby." Joshua could tell by how tense her body became, that there was some vital information that she was intentionally dodging.

Shaking her head, "I can't do this with you Sug!"

"Baby, I need you to trust me enough to tell me." Joshua didn't know what qualified him to be heroic enough to battle her demons. But, the way being in her presence made him feel, he would sure as hell try.

Carla positioned her hand over her eyes and attempted to gather her thoughts. "He cheated on me. Constantly. He was so good at lying and playing games that it became hard to distinguish the truth from a lie. I went into my Private Investigator mode. Some call it call stalking, but I call it being resourceful."

"Everything that I allowed myself to become blind too, surfaced." Carla continued to explain. "There were females everywhere with loads of gifts, money and expensive possessions. Dre paid all the bills in our home so our money affairs were none of my concern until then."

"Do you still love him?" Joshua interjected.

"Of course, I love him, but I'm not in love with him. When I filed for legal separation I was eleven weeks pregnant. I was so stressed out Sug." Before she could stop them, tears were streaming down Carla's face and Joshua was trying to catch them. "I miscarried, the cramping started off as just discomfort and it increased extremely. I went to the bathroom and there was so much blood, by the time my sister got me to the hospital, the finishing stages of the miscarriage wasn't complete. But, I was certain the baby was gone and the doctors couldn't find the heart-beat."

"I'm sorry babe, I'm so sorry." Holding her close so that she could feel the warmth and sincerity of his words. Joshua felt like shit asking her to go into detail, but he had to know, he had feelings for her and he didn't want to begin a relationship that would soon come to an end.

When she had composed herself enough to finish, Carla continued. "He had three other women pregnant besides me, one baby was still-born, one chick miscarried at sixteen weeks and the other got an abortion. And after all of that shit you would think that he would be kind enough to let me out of this marriage without so much hassle. After a while, I just stopped mentioning the divorce to him altogether."

"Do you still talk to him?" Joshua asked further.

Smiling, "Yes, I talk to his crazy ass, we're actually good friends again, it's been almost five years since everything's happened. He still wants us to work it out, but I'm not real interested. He never came to the hospital when I miscarried or when I had to have an emergency D& C procedure." Seeing the sympathetic look in Joshua's eyes, Carla snuggled against his chest while he rubbed her back in a soothing motion.

"You don't have to tell me anymore CeCe, I shouldn't have forced you too!"

Drawing back from him, Carla assured, "Trust me if I didn't want to tell you, I wouldn't have. I feel like if it was imperative for you to know, then I wanted to share it with you. Since the separation, I haven't met anyone worth pushing for the divorce so I left it as a dead issue."

"So is your last name Williams or is it Davis?"

"Its Williams, I never changed it to Davis." Carla confessed.

"Don't you believe in a woman submitting to a man whole-heartedly and doing him the ultimate honor of taking his last name?"

"That little gift I told you about earlier; I just could sense that something wasn't right after we got married and shortly all hell broke loose, so I never changed it."

"Alright." Kissing the top of her head, "Enough with the heavy stuff, you want to watch a movie or something?" Joshua exhausted the conversation.

"We can see what's already on TV; I know we're going to be sleep soon."

"Is that what you think?" He asked.

"It's what I hope; I don't want you dwelling on what I told you tonight, I don't want it to ruin me being here with you." Carla started to remove her legs from around Joshua's body when he grabbed her and plastered her into him until her butt was in his lap and hoisted under his hands. Sitting on top of him gave Carla about an inch above his frame, leaving her to look down into his eyes with him staring up.

"Don't be like that; you and I are good! Everybody has a past and I haven't passed any judgment. I just want to understand you so that I can interact with you in a way that doesn't make you so defensive and eliminates you pushing me away."

Looking into his deep dark eyes, "I feel safe with you!" Carla admitted.

"Do you?"

"Yes."

"Good, never be around a man who doesn't make you feel safe." Joshua met Carla halfway and sealed the unspoken truth with a kiss. He laid Carla down on the right side of the bed with his hand underneath her breast, so that they were at an angle to see the television.

Holding onto his arms, she murmured, "Can I tell you something?"

Joshua held her as close to him as he could get her, "Anything!"

"My worst fear is not being able to carry a baby." Carla confessed.

Angling his head down so that he could whisper in her ear, "I think you're more than capable of carrying a baby and if you want me to prove it to you, I have no problem with that either!"

Tickled and shocked at his comment, "I'll keep that in mind!"

He searched through the channels and when he finally found something suitable, he noticed that Carla's breathing had deepened and she was sound asleep.

This was the second time that Joshua had the pleasure of watching her sleep, the first time had been her first night in Chicago. She was a pretty woman and he admired the strength that she showed, even after everything that her husband had put her through. Joshua was determined that she didn't have to portray a hard front with him, that it was a man's job to do the battling, not for them to battle against each other.

Chapter 10

Waking up the next morning to the smell of breakfast, Carla temporarily forgot where she was until she turned over and Joshua's cologne scent was embedded in the pillows. Going into the bathroom to brush her teeth and wash her face. She crept into the kitchen to find Joshua dancing to old school music; he was doing an imitation of the moonwalk with a spatula in his hand.

"Is this what I can look forward too when I stay the night at your house?" Carla interrupted.

Caught off guard, Joshua spun around. "I can also drop a hook or two, but if you repeat it outside of this house, this is going to be your last visit."

Giggling and moving closer, Carla kissed and hugged him. "He raps and dances, well Good Morning!"

"Morning Sug. How did you sleep?"

"It was perfect!" She wasn't sure if he called her Sug to please her or if his feelings towards her were changing to mirror how she felt.

"Good, I made a little breakfast with turkey sausage and bacon." Giving Carla a sideways glance.

"I'm not against turkey products." She informed him.

"Sit down and I'll make a plate for you."

Once both of them were seated at the table, Carla went right in for the kill. "So why do you have four children, three baby mother's, but no wife?"

Shaking his head, Joshua should have known it would be his turn to stand in the line of fire, just not this soon. "I never found a woman to marry; I have cheated on every woman that I have ever been with up until the last five years."

"Should I be worried?" Suddenly Carla wasn't so hungry.

"No, I have made it a practice to work on my self-respect and only sleep with one woman at a time. For the last five years it has worked and I have conceded and examined that sex is only 70% mental."

"Interesting." Carla murmured.

"Stop It. You asked me a question and I answered it. I want to be honest with you and I want to keep the lines of communication open." Joshua's face hardened slightly.

"Okay." Throwing her hands up in a surrendering stance. "I like the sound of that!" Carla answered.

Finishing breakfast, they got dressed and headed downtown for some sightseeing. Just being in his presence made Carla's days better while in Chicago and she wondered if Joshua could be the one who would make her consider filing for a divorce. Even though Carla and Dre were back to the friend zone of their relationship she was no longer interested in a marriage with him. Dre had broken her heart and trust and she was hesitant to give anyone else that kind of power again.

September 14, 2012

Carla couldn't believe it, thirty days had passed and she was on her third training class. Everyone had grasped the concepts and transitioned smoothly from Humility to Serenity's operating systems. Things were wonderful between Joshua and her, his mood swings had turned into rocking motions just as Taylor predicted, but sex was still a non-factor for them. Carla was convinced that it definitely wasn't the chemistry because when he held her at night, dew wasn't the only thing evident in the morning.

Carla had returned to Michigan September 2, 2012, to spend Labor Day weekend with her family and Joshua accompanied her. Reacquainting himself with the family was quite easy, although Carla's father Carlos, wasn't as warm and receptive this time. Once Carla and Carlos were alone, he let it be known his position on her and the older man. He reasoned that Joshua hadn't married the mothers of his children and there was a great possibility that the outcome would be the same for her. As her father spoke, Carla recapped on the revelation she found through Joshua's Zodiac sign and what Aries men were known for.

But, as quickly as the conversation with her father came to mind, Carla dismissed it. She was almost thirty-years-old and even though she respected and cherished her father's opinion, it wasn't one that would rule or dictate her life or actions.

Packing up her belongings for the day; it was Friday and all Carla wanted to do was crawl under Joshua for the remainder of the evening. Walking towards Joshua's car, he unlocked the doors and took one look at her face and knew there would be no sexual healing tonight.

"What's the matter Sug?"

Slouching over the armrest and grabbing his warm slender, long hands, she placed them on her stomach.

"You're on your period babe?" Joshua rubbed her stomach in a circular motion.

Carla laid her head on his shoulder. "I don't want to stop you from going out with the team today; you can drop me off at the hotel." She felt Joshua's hand go still.

"Are you trying to piss me off? Why would I leave you?" Kissing the top of her head, he ran his hands through her hair. Joshua was going to utilize the night to be what she needed, since she had come into his world and became what he needed most at the time he had least expected it.

The laughter had returned in his eyes and he was well-aware that the warmth that exuded off of him when Carla was near was because she provided him with that. Joshua had been content with the emptiness that he had accepted years ago and the only thing that was deemed as a shining light were his youth that he had produced.

Following his orders, Carla sunk down in the seat and closed her eyes to find some comfort and peace in the 800mgh Motrin that she swallowed earlier.

Breaking her serene atmosphere that she had created, Joshua asked. "Is there anything that you need before we go to the house? Pain pills, juice, food?"

"I'm okay, I just want to lie down for a bit and give the medicine I took some time to work." She was going to ask him what he knew about women, periods, cramps and medicine, but she guessed now wasn't the time to start. But of course, he had seventeen years of experience on her.

"You've had too many encounters with women and menstrual cycles!" She blurted.

Cocking his head and looking at her through the slit of eyes he said, "I was messing with women, way before your mama had the chance to understand the concept of having a period."

Laughing at his unorthodox comment about her mama she went back to her meditating position, "I'll be sure to let her know!"

Walking into his house, Joshua took off his shoes after Carla and made his way to the bathroom as she went in the direction of the bedroom. He rolled up the cuffs on his dress shirt and ran some water in the tub that wasn't scorching, but too hot to be considered warm. He headed back towards his bedroom and found Carla laid on her side, fully clothed. Climbing onto the bed in front of her while standing on his knees, he began unbuttoning her blazer when her eyes opened.

He leaned over and kissed her lips, "I'm making you a bath, it should help. Has the medicine kicked in yet?"

"Yes it has." Carla was slightly filled with relief. Joshua was unaware that hot baths were a remedy that she used for her period. Not that it made the pain go away, but it relaxed her muscles enough to endure it! Lifting her body to assist with the removal of her jacket; he began to unbutton her blouse. Brushing it off of her shoulders, he reached behind her to unzip her skirt, allowing it and her panty hose to skate down her legs. The intimate act left Carla with only her bra and panties still in place.

She could see the gentleness and lust in his eyes as her body burned with heat. *Did he seriously just undress me while he was still fully clothed?* Inclining her head to the side, "I think you should turn the water off Babe." Watching Joshua retreat to the bathroom gave Carla a moment for herself to just breathe, another few minutes of his hands on her and she was going to turn into a ball of flames.

Strolling back into the bedroom, Joshua hovered near Carla with the look of lust still raging in his eyes. She allowed his hands to travel along the center of her body, until they rested between the crack of her ass and her spine. "I love your body Babe, you have no idea how much I wished your period had held off a few more days."

Smiling Carla enveloped his waist with her arms and clutched further into his grip and whispered, "I know!" Kissing his lips slowly and pulling away before he could deepen the kiss as she walked into the bathroom.

"Let me know when you're settled in and I'll come and wash your back." Joshua knew that he was full of shit, but what else could he do? The girl was already under his skin and seeing her half naked had damn near drove him off the edge that he had been patiently sitting on.

After ten minutes had passed, he knocked on the door, "Babe you good?"

"I'm okay!"

"Can I come in?"

There was a brief pause before Carla replied, "Sure."

Joshua slowly opened the door, Carla automatically noticed that he had traded his suit and tie for some gray jogging pants, that hung off of his slender hips and a white t-shirt with house shoes. He kneeled at the foot of the tub, "How does it feel?"

"It's just what I needed." Carla had covered her chest with her chin resting on her knees.

"Are you hiding your body from me Mami'?" He asked.

Knowing that lying was not her strong suit, she went in for the truth. "That's a possibility, Sug!"

"I know you're not afraid of me, but I know that the dynamics change when you go from being fully clothed to naked." Leaning in to Carla, Joshua placed his lips on her chin and slowly nipped it, following the trail of her jaw line. Stretching her legs into the water, he could hear the sharp intake of her breath, as he traveled down her neck. Carla tilted her head further to the right to give him more access.

With his free hand he parted her legs and felt her drawback, "I got you Sug, I promise." He whispered and looked into her eyes as he closed in to kiss her. Waiting until he deepened the kiss to feel her hunger before he returned to slipping his hand between her thighs.

Joshua wanted to make sure that Carla felt some of the lust that he had been battling, when his middle finger skimmed over her clit, it exposed that she was just as excited. Carla pulled back slightly and he breathed into her mouth, "I got you Sug!"

She lifted her hand out of the water and placed it on the back on Joshua's hand, "I don't want you to put your fingers in me, I just came on remember?"

"Mami' I know how to make you cum without putting my fingers inside of you, I got it Baby, I got it!"

She was just as experienced as the next single woman when it came to masturbation, but it was definitely more pleasurable to have him do it. She initiated the kiss this time, while rising on her knees to shift her opening towards the side of the tub, spreading her thighs like a butterfly.

This time he broke the kiss, "You gon fuck around and I'm going to join you in this tub and it won't be my fingers plunging into you or stimulating your clit."

On her knees she dragged him closer, with the only thing separating them being the molding of the tub. She was fully exposed as his mouth found her nipples, gently sucking and tugging as her body betrayed her and her fingers tangled and gripped his neck. "Babe." Carla moaned, "Babe."

Knowing that there was no turning back, Joshua moved to the other breast and performed the same favor while he moved his hand back to her core. It was sticking out validating her arousal, she was beyond ready for him. Moving his hand up and down the tender piece of flesh, he heard her grit her teeth as she tightened the hold on his neck. He continued to tug on her chocolate nipples that were completely stirred and at his disposal.

Stroking her clit in a spherical motion, working his mouth up her neck and landing on her lips, he knew it wouldn't be long before it was over. "I want to see you cum for me Baby. Can you do that for Daddy, cum for me?" He moved a hand over her breast, allowing her body to find a rhythm with his fingers. When her head fell back, he increased the pressure on the mound as well as the speed of his motion that he was rousing deep in her walls.

She couldn't stop the trimmers and convulsions as her body gave in to the pleasure. The evidence flowed slowly between her legs and it was confirmed, she had cum for him.

Opening her eyes while concurrently lowering her body back into the cooling water, "You definitely cheated." She accused.

"Did I? I think your body would disagree with you. I just wanted you to know what's in store for you."

"I hope that you understand that payback is a bitch." Carla playfully splashed the water.

"Indeed." Grabbing her towel and lathering it with soap, Joshua proceeded to wash her body from head to toe, leaving her to tend to the more sensitive body parts.

Carla rinsed off, exited the tub, put on a pad and some underwear and slid into a long t-shirt. Joshua traded his jogging pants for boxers and extended his arms for her to join him. He had never wanted to be inside a woman so badly, never yearned to be near a woman so badly. And it was silently starting to piss him off; it was illogical how he felt for her without being inside of her yet. He comprehended that he shouldn't have compared his emotions to sex, but he was still a man. Although he controlled his thought process the older he had become, sometimes he couldn't ignore his male anatomy's logic.

Carla didn't lay down with him, but straddled him, with a leg on each side of his body and a glistening look in her eyes, "Sug, I love everything about you!" She exclaimed.

He didn't know what to say because the truth was he was falling for her too, but instead of communicating that he replied. "You don't know enough about me to love it?"

Faintly offended she leaned up, "I know enough! But you can tell me so that I can understand you better!"

Elevating her legs to settle on the bed rather than on his crotch, but Joshua stopped her in the midst of it, settling her body back, "Don't get up." He knew he had offended her, but he wanted to be honest with her. A man like him didn't deserve the love inside of her or the love she wanted to give him.

"Okay, I won't get up, but I want you to explain the things that you believe that I need to know in order to make a full assessment of how much I do or don't feel for you."

He adjusted his body against the head-board of the bed. Joshua wasn't an open man; he didn't walk around exploiting his younger years, indiscretions and countless mistakes. He was man enough to admit that he made rash decisions, but Carla was one decision that he wouldn't regret, nor would he forget. She was a breath of fresh air and he appreciated what she was generous enough to add to his life. He wondered if he could trust her enough to share some of his darkest demons.

"CeCe, I was a playa long before I became a man and some of the choices that I made caused my children to suffer as the end result. Their lifestyles and choices that they've exercised are partially because I wasn't there for them in the capacity that they needed."

Cutting in, Carla jumped to his defense. "You were fifteen, how were you supposed to care for two children? How could you have guided them in an appropriate manner and equip them for life when you didn't know the first thing about it yourself? You were barely a teenager."

Smiling, "You seem to have the answers for everything, huh?"

"Well the reality is that I'm well beyond my years and the reality is that you aren't just attracted to me because I'm pretty, but definitely because I can hold my own."

"You sure have a concrete opinion of what the reality is to only be twenty-eight. Babe you haven't even began to explore life yet. You're going to grow and change a whole lot more before you turn thirty, again when you turn thirty-five and for sure when forty comes knocking on your door."

Carla tried not to become agitated, "I'm not sure if you're trying to aggravate me or enlighten me, but I'll do us both a favor and grant you the benefit of a doubt."

"Excuse me?" He asked.

"Yes, the benefit of the doubt."

"I'm not real familiar with the term, elaborate!"

Was this grown ass man shitting her, was he pulling her leg or had his choices in life caused him to draw a wall where the benefit of the doubt wasn't an option for him? "Umm." Carla was thrown off by having to explain this concept. "It means that although the scenario, answer or result may not be clear or convincing, you trust me enough to take my word over what's being presented." She exceeded in her explanation.

"There's that trust word again. Yeah, we aren't exactly on a first name basis," Joshua explained. "Trust and I were like a one night stand. She came for what she wanted, I got what I needed and when we were finished handling business, she stole everything I had, including the clothes on my back."

Smiling at his metaphor, "That's an intriguing mechanism for describing your relationship with Trust. But I'm definitely not going to hurt you. I'll be your safe haven . . . your place of refuge."

With his lip caressing the side of her neck, he held her with a locked grip, "You make me feel so many emotions and from the moment I met you, I've been trying to avoid dealing with them, but somehow you give me a reason not to push you away."

"It's because you love me too!" Without realizing what she said, it was too late and Carla couldn't take it back.

Lifting his head and staring in her eyes, "You love me Sug?"

Trying to clean up her statement and shifting her gaze, "Of course, I love everything about you!"

"Loving everything about me and saying, 'I Love You' is not the same and I know you're intelligent enough to comprehend that." Grabbing her by the chin to redirect her focus back to him.

"I didn't say I love you though." Carla explained.

"No, but you said too, which implies that you love me."

"Maybe we should explore the fact that you haven't denied that you loved me either!" Carla flipped the script.

"And maybe I won't."

"Then say it!"

"I'll say it once I'm inside of you!" He stated.

Looking for any kind of distraction Carla spun off Joshua's lap and began fixing the bed to retire for the night. "The convo is getting a little too heavy for me; can we pick this back up in the morning or next week or something?" Carla asked.

Snickering, "Yeah baby that's fine." Joshua felt her body relax and heard the deep sigh that came from within the pit of her stomach as he tightened his hold. There was so much he wanted her to know about him, about his life before he restructured it, but now just wasn't the time.

CHAPTER 11

$\mathscr{A}$t the mercy of her bladder, Carla woke to use the bathroom glancing at the clock on the night stand; it read 3:37AM. She conjured a wonderful idea in light of the events that had occurred the night before and she re-entered the bathroom to brush her teeth.

Hiking on the bed and trying to be as light as possible so that she wouldn't risk waking Joshua. Carla slowly pulled the covers back and slipped her hand in the opening of his boxers and grabbed the limp yet lengthy penis in her hands causing a sleeping Joshua to stir. "Baby what are you doing?"

Not bothering to answer his question with words, she lowered her head in between his thighs and took his growing penis into her mouth one inch at a time. She started with the head as it slid passed her teeth and washed over her tongue, eliciting a moan from him. Carla was more enthused that he seemed to be enjoying himself as she inched more of him towards her throat. Looking up at him as his powerful instrument slid in and out of her mouth, she found a rhythm.

At that moment, the air was thick with passion and yearning and she wanted nothing more than to show him what he meant to her. Her desired outcome was for her to thoroughly please him and since her body was out of commission, she would use her mouth.

Allowing her mouth to overflow with saliva and drip down his shaft, it provided the opportunity for her to slowly stroke the now wet skin with her hand while simultaneously moving her tongue over the head. Pushing passed her limits and allowing it to touch the back of her throat when she heard him cry out!

Joshua thrust his hands into her hair and used her head as the key component in the instrumental piece that they were creating. He gave up, she won, his scrotum tightened, his dick was at full attention and he knew if Carla closed her lips around him for another ten seconds, he was finished.

Before he could react or respond, Carla pulled his heavy, lengthy and full erection out of her mouth replacing it with her palm as she milked him with four closed palm pumps. Joshua squirted a load of cum in the air, on his stomach, legs and her hands with a groan hollow enough to be mistaken as a wounded animal.

Joshua paralleled her over his body and whispered, "Bay are you crazy?" Blinking as if he were trying to correct his vision.

Carla knew she'd thrown him for a loop, but her only reply was, "I told you that payback was a bitch!"

Smiling, he yanked and kissed her hard on the mouth, "I don't know what I'm going to do with you!"

"I could think of a few things!" Carla suggested.

Joshua maneuvered to the bathroom where he turned on the water and grabbed his wash cloth to erase the evidence of what transpired. He'd be lying if he said that she hadn't rocked his world and surprised the hell out of him, but he did have one question. Walking towards the bedroom, "Sug?"

"Yes love!"

"You don't swallow?" Joshua asked.

Catching her by surprise and temporarily leaving her mute. Joshua continued with his pursuit, "Mami' you don't swallow?" He had a full beam on, showing every tooth in his mouth as he laid down on the bed.

"Umm, swallow, hmmm!"

The amusement that was bubbling at the back of Joshua's throat became a full, hearty laugh that was unmistakably from his diaphragm. "After you just did, what you just did, I know you're not getting shy on me?"

Crawling on the bed making her way over to where he stood, "I have never swallowed!"

"Ever?"

Smiling at his amazement, "Ever!" Bumping her forehead against his.

Joshua kissed her lips, "Baby?"

"Hmm?"

Kissing her lips again, "I want you to swallow!"

She kissed him back, "I'll think about it!"

"Hmm okay, while you're thinking, tell me how you learned to do it so good?"

"HA! Do you watch porn?"

"No, I draw the line at strip clubs."

"Well my husband loved them and it rubbed off on me, so I watch them regularly and they can teach you a thing or two."

"Yea okay!"

"I'm sure you'd be grateful for what I've learned." Smirking and snuggling back under the covers.

Saturday Afternoon Joshua began preparing to make Lasagna and garlic bread and Carla sat at the kitchen table to keep him company. As long as he didn't mind cooking then she didn't mind watching.

"My daughters are coming into town in two weeks and I want you to meet them!"

"Um, okay." Diverting her eyes from his face to the table.

"What's the matter?"

Carla rose from the table "Nothing, I need to use the bathroom!"

Joshua grabbed her arm before she could walk pass him, "Wait, tell me!"

"Nothing!"

"You're lying!" He accused.

Huffing and puffing, Carla blurted. "I'm afraid to meet your daughters!"

"Why?"

"Well for one, we're in the same age category. For two, you and I are seventeen years apart AND I just gave their father a blow job last night!"

Lifting her chin to meet his gaze, "Babe, my daughters are cool, they're not like that!"

"You don't understand because you're not a daughter. I would kill any female that was my age and thought she could date my dad. My sisters and I would be waiting on her ass with gym shoes and Vaseline."

Laughing out loud, "Babe, you're so serious!"

"Sug, I'm dead serious, it's a chick so hood that lives inside of me. She isn't a hoe about her shit at all!" Gesturing ghetto hand movements and laughing with him.

Looking into to her eyes, "I do love you!" Joshua uttered.

Right then at that moment, Carla's world stood still. "Sug! I thought you weren't going to say it until you were inside me?"

"I don't know when I'm going to be inside you, but it felt like the right time to say it!"

"Are you feeling some kind of way because you haven't gotten any ass, but we constantly sleep in the same bed?" Carla inquired.

"My grandfather use to have this saying; he would say . . . . naw, nevermind."

"No tell me, I want to know!"

"You really want to know?"

"Yes!"

"He would tell me not to fuck all the hoes!"

"Huh?" Carla asked puzzled.

Joshua laughed at her surprised reaction.

"Elaborate Sug!" Carla requested.

"It just means that you should always have someone who matters and that you haven't treated like the rest!"

"Should I assume that you're asking me to be that girl?"

"Maybe I am! But I want you to know that the kind of lifestyle that I lived didn't allow me to pretend or play-dumb with my daughters, so not putting them up on game wasn't an option."

"What kind of life have you lived?"

"A life in the streets and doing what I had to do to take care of my family. When the ends didn't meet, I had to do what was necessary to stay afloat."

Trying to probe gently, Carla asked. "Can you tell me what life in the streets consisted of?"

Joshua glared at Carla as if she had three eyes, "I just told you that it meant doing whatever was necessary!"

"But, why not get in school? Get a regular job?"

Smirking for the first time, Joshua gleefully informed Carla, "I used the money to put myself through school. My looks and many talents didn't afford me this head trainer position. I busted my ass to climb the corporate latter to get where I am now. I earned a Bachelor's Degree in Leadership Education at the University of Pennsylvania."

Carla flashed him a million dollar smile, "How long have you been out of the streets?"

Joshua used his fingers to calculate the distance his forty-five years on earth had traveled, "Ten years! The first five years were the hardest. I was trying to avoid indulging in certain activities and that's why my respect for monogamy is so recent. The second five years were easier, but it's so easy to relapse so I try to take it one day at a time."

Carla found her voice, "That's all you can do Jay!"

Carla was at a loss of words for the first time since their initial meeting. She should have known by the edge that he possessed along with those eyes that were beyond nonsense. Joshua's ability to shut down completely and ignore her as if she never existed, was indescribable. What had she gotten herself into? Whatever it was, she wasn't ready to walk away from it yet.

CHAPTER 12

September 24, 2012

The week and weekend had gone by without many complications and Joshua's daughters were expected to arrive Friday, that gave Carla four days to prepare. Carla was still just as nervous as the first time that he mentioned their visit, but there was something else nagging at her. Something was seriously wrong or headed in the wrong direction, but she couldn't put her finger on it so she would sweep it under the rug for now.

The knock at the training classroom door shifted Carla's thoughts to the back of her mind. Looking up she seen him, "Hey Babe."

"Hey Sug. Are you about ready to head out of here?"

"No, not yet. There are some things I need to edit and prepare for tomorrow's class."

"Okay, so you want to do a late dinner? Maybe like 9pm?"

"Oh, that's real late, but yeah I should home by then!"

Bending down to kiss her, Joshua headed for the door to leave the building for the day. When he arrived home an eerie feeling swept over him as if something was out of place. Before he could take the shoes off his feet and hang his suit jacket up, there was a knock at the door. Checking the peephole, he couldn't recognize the face.

Opening the door his heart dropped and the worst scenario's came to mind, "Breanne?"

"Hi Jay, how are you?" Breanne replied.

"It depends on what you came all the way to Chicago to tell me? Is everything okay? Did someone die?"

"I'm sorry to drop in on you like this. Can I come in and I'll explain?"

Back at the hotel, Carla was starting to pace her hotel room. It was 8:30pm and she had called and texted Joshua with no response. She was in between a rock and a hard place on what she thought was the best thing to do. Should she wait for his call or text or should she just show up at his place unannounced? Even though she spent a great deal of time there, Carla didn't live there. She didn't have keys and he wasn't officially her man. But, that eerie feeling she had been fighting for days was back and in full effect.

When 9pm came around, she received a text from Joshua stating that he was sorry, but he was going to have to cancel dinner and that he would see her at work in the morning.

When Carla replied to ask if everything was ok, she never received a response.

Strutting into work bright and early Tuesday morning, Carla was on edge. She was tired and emotionally spent. She had spent the entire night praying that everything was ok, but knowing that whatever was to happen next would be inevitable.

Making her way to her desk and logging into the system, she surfed the internet. Carla had approximately thirty-five minutes before she was to head to her classroom. Logging into her Facebook account, she decided to do a little research on Joshua's daughters. Her motto was to have the upper hand regardless of who it was because she was not going to be cornered by Jayla and Jasmine Williams.

Jayla seemed fairly ordinary with smooth caramel skin and distinctive features that mirrored Joshua's, but nothing alarming jumped out at Carla regarding her. Surfing over to Jasmine's page there was some familiarity there. Carla tried to place her face, but couldn't quite put her finger on where she had seen her before. Jasmine possessed a sexiness that ranged high above the average twenty-five year old. Jasmine was a half of shade darker than Jayla with more defined features in the cheekbones, but she also looked like Joshua.

Carla was mature enough to admit that she had an animal instinct since the tender age of six that never led her astray. Out of Joshua's four children, the only one that she wasn't able to locate on Facebook, Twitter or Instagram was Jonathan. There were so many thoughts running through Carla's mind, but the first thing she needed to do was deal with Joshua and the bullshit he handed her lastnight.

It wasn't quite 8am yet, so she was sure that Joshua wasn't at his desk. Confused on what to do next, Carla placed a text to her sister Chrissey for some guidance. Chrissey wasn't your typical younger sister, she picked up some street sense in the womb and nobody could uncover dirt like she could. Putting her phone away and logging off the system, it was time for Carla to start her day. She would have to deal with Joshua later.

When lunchtime came, Carla cornered Joshua at his desk. "Hey You!"

When Joshua looked up, he remembered why he had been dodging Carla, he knew that she was able to pick up on things. And the last thing he needed was her drilling into his brain. "Hey CeCe, what's up?"

Stepping closer, "CeCe, huh?"

Smirking, "Mami' what's up?"

"That's a little better; you tell me what's up?"

"Nothing, you want to get some lunch?" Joshua asked, dodging the subject.

"No, I want you to tell me what happened last night!"

Joshua's muscles were as stiff as cardboard, "Nothing Babe, I just wasn't feeling well!"

Bending down and getting real close to his face, Carla warned. "I dare you to lie to my face again!"

Joshua chuckled. "Are you threatening me? You better chill out and let me feed your ass, before we tear this mothafuckin building up!" Standing to his feet and grabbing her arm, Joshua ushered her from the front door of the building to the passenger seat of his truck.

She could have put up a fight, but she just didn't want too, she liked when he talked to her like that! It turned her on in ways one couldn't explain.

CHAPTER 13

For the next two days, Joshua was a hermit and she was determined that she wouldn't nag him because she wasn't going to force anyone to spend time with her. Carla refused to turn into the girl who was insanely in love with a man who was old enough to be her father.

She had spent the last two consecutive nights in her hotel room and she would make do with that. There was a possibility that the situation was going to get out of hand and it was as if Carla could feel the bullshit beginning to boil in her blood. Joshua was hiding something, but he didn't have to worry about her prying into his thoughts because she wasn't so sure that she wanted to know.

Glancing at her phone, Carla saw a text from Dre that asked when he could see her. But, Carla ignored the message just as she had done for the past several weeks. She was hoping that Dre would get tired of her giving him the cold shoulder and disappear.

It was Thursday afternoon and the manager that was assigned to Carla allowed her to leave early since her class moved swiftly through the session's assignment. This was a brighter group that she worked with and tomorrow they would complete their assessment.

Hearing a knock at her hotel door, Carla wasn't cognizant of the fact that she had fallen asleep. She stretched the muscles in her arms and legs and rotated her neck from side to side cracking the tension that resonated. She was more tired than she thought and the sun had set and evening was approaching with every second that Carla remained in the bed. When she stayed the night at Joshua's they didn't have sex, but she tossed the entire night from inhaling and dreaming of him. His masculine fragrance of soap and laundry detergent was entangled in every sense that she owned and it usually left her captive and intoxicated.

Sluggishly uprooting her body off of the bed and stumbling towards the door, she glanced in the peephole and she didn't know whether to be happy or upset. Today was day three and he had massive balls showing up like everything was gravy.

Cracking the door enough to hear what he wanted, but not enough for Joshua to assume that Carla was ushering him in the suite.

"I know you're upset!" Joshua insisted.

"I'm not sure what gave you that impression!" Carla commented dismissively.

Moving closer to the entrance, he rested his head in the peep of the door, close enough for her to feel his breath, but far enough that he couldn't touch her.

"Baby." He exhaled. "I have had a hell of a week, one hell of a day and now its boiling down to the hours. Please let me in! I just want hold you because I don't have the strength to fight."

Sucking her teeth, Carla was agitated, how was she supposed to remain mad at him when he sounded like that and said things of that sort. Snatching the door open, "I can't deal with your mood swings, especially when I can feel it. Do you know how annoying that is? Not only do I have to deal with my own emotional ass, I have to sort out your mess too."

Joshua didn't care that she was fussing; it would be awhile before he'd be able to hear her do it again, so he would relish her wrath. Walking towards her as if she hadn't said a word and locking his arms around her with his head in the crook of her neck. "I need you!"

Carla had never seen him like this before, vulnerable and open. She didn't know what to do, but to give him what he seemed to need from her. "I'm here Babe, what's the matter?"

Joshua lifted her and Carla encircled her legs around his waist. Joshua walked towards the bed and placed her in the middle of it, allowing his body to follow hers into the mattress. Immediately, she could feel the tension and desire travel through his body and she quickly understood what he meant by the words, *I need you!*

Joshua's kisses were hard and needy, but soothed to gentle and coaxing. He knew Carla's blood had to be scorching because he was close to combusting. If he stopped now then he wouldn't go through with it because of the intensity of his own need had rocked him to the core.

Balancing his body weight over hers, he began to explore the rest of her body. He searched her eyes for any indication that this wasn't what she wanted and that she didn't crave him in the capacity that he longed for her. When he found none, he unbuttoned her blouse and slid it off of her shoulders. Taking her right nipple and then her left into his mouth, Joshua was tugging, suckling and probing it to become harder, when he heard her gasp. Knowing that it had been years since Carla had let a man into her body, he needed to ensure that she was soft enough to accommodate his length.

Sliding his hands down her body and resting them on her pelvis, he couldn't seem to get close enough to her. Undoing the buttons on her slacks and hooking his fingers in the waist band of her pants, he stepped back to slither them pass her thighs and down her legs.

The lacy lingerie underwear matched the bra that he had long discarded. Not wanting to wait much longer, he glided his pants and boxers off in one motion. The hunger was more apparent in his hardened flesh as he journeyed back in between Carla's legs. He used his thumb to play with her clit and then the head of his penis as her moaning sky-rocketed in his ear. "Baby, I won't enter you until I know that your body can accept me without hurting you!"

Carla couldn't find the words to say anything so she nodded that she understood. She also comprehended that his appetite was born out of whatever it was that he wasn't willing to share with her. But, she loved him enough to allow him to work it out inside of her. She was tired of the distance between them and the crashing waves rafting his moody attitude.

His mouth discarded every thought that was going through Carla's mind. She arched her back as his tongue slid over her sensitive clitoris. Joshua held his arms around her hips to keep her in place as he skillfully placed the demand on her body to cum for him. Carla clenched her hands in the sheets to stop herself from grabbing the back of head and pushing it further into her frontal lips. He was making love to her pussy; kissing, sucking, licking and caressing the most feminine part of her while plunging his index finger into her hot and dripping opening.

Her body gave up the ghost and she couldn't hold on any longer when Joshua pulled his finger out and added his middle finger to re-enter her again.

Whispering hoarsely, "Babe. Babe, I'm about to—." She couldn't get the words off her tongue, when the shaking in her thighs increased and her walls erupted, permitting her juices to seep out.

Traveling up the length of her body. "Sug, I know I got pussy juice on my lips, but I really need to kiss you!"

Giggling at his forward comment, Carla initiated the kiss, bracing herself for what was sure to come next.

Joshua pushed his left hand into her hair as he grinded his penis against her folds, Carla draped her legs around his back to grant him access. Deepening the kiss, Joshua guided the head inside her slit just enough for Carla to break the kiss with a gasp. Joshua stiffened and responded to how tightly closed her vagina was.

Joshua asked, "How much of me will your body accept?"

Moaning at the slight movement he made inside of her, she breathed. "All of it!"

"All of it?" Joshua tried to confirm.

Carla's breathing turned into panting. "Yes Baby, all of it." Dropping her hands to caress his hips, "She'll stretch for you!"

He hovered over her and slipped another inch inside until more than half of him was drenched in the confines of her body.

Using his expertise in the field to make her more comfortable, Joshua tenderly began moving in and out of her, causing her moans to escalate and his penis to overflow with moisture. He was trying to drag out this love scene as long as possible for Carla, but he was losing his mind inside of her. With every stroke he was falling deeper in love with her, dreading the outcome that was inevitable. If he never wanted to execute being a gentleman before, he would tonight. Joshua was going to hold out until Carla received what her body had been neglecting.

Executing a light thrust and feeling her vagina tighten and grab his dick deeper, Joshua quickened his pace. He felt her arch her back and half moan/half cry as she neared her orgasm, he was going to cum with her. With his stomach clenching and his scrotum drawing up, he whispered. "Oh God Baby, let it go, please let it go!" At his plea, her body exploded and she milked every piece of nut he seemed to have lingering, leaving them both spent.

When Joshua looked up at Carla, her eyes were still closed. "Baby, you okay?"

Her only reply was, "Umm Hmm!"

He knew that she was going to be sore and he wanted her comfortable before he talked to her. Getting up from the bed, he went and ran her a warm bath. Skating back into the bedroom, he kissed Carla's closed eyes. "I want you to soak a little bit in the tub, CeCe."

Stirring enough to reply. "But, I don't want to move!"

Bending down and scooping her up, he placed her in the bath tub. "I'll grab you some towels."

"Mmm k!" Was the only response that she could muster.

Returning to the bathroom, he found a sleeping Carla. Taking the face cloth, he lathered it and began washing her body, starting with her shoulders. "Was it that good Babe?"

Giggling, "You are so full of yourself."

"I mean you damn near drowned in the tub, I'm just asking." Joshua smiled.

Laughing out loud, "You are something else." Opening her eyes and staring up at him for the first time. "It was that good, but I believe that it's your energy that you were so kind to transfer to me, that has me exhausted. Do you feel better?" Carla asked him.

Rubbing his hand over her cheek, "I'm sorry about that." Joshua moved in for a kiss. "I do feel better though Bay."

"I'm glad that I could offer some assistance." Carla removed the towel from his fingers and lathered it more to wash and rinse her soft spots.

"Once you get out the tub, I'll take a shower."

Thirty minutes later, Joshua crawled into bed with Carla. "Babe, I need to talk to you!"

Carla turned in his embrace. "I'm listening; I've been waiting on you to tell me for days!" She confessed while rubbing her hands down his lean, but built chest.

Joshua rested his forehead against hers. "I have to leave town tomorrow!"

"Huh? Where are you going?"

"Pennsylvania."

"What's going on in Pennsylvania?"

Joshua knew that she was going to drill him with questions and that's why he held on to the information as long as possible. "Can you trust me to tell you when I have all of the answers?"

Carla pushed out of his grasp. "Babe, this isn't making much sense. When are you coming back?"

Joshua pulled her back close to him. "Hopefully Sunday night, but right now I need you to trust me. Can you do that?"

"I don't know. Can I do that? Should I do that?" She quizzed him.

"I haven't given you a reason not to trust me since I met you. I don't have all the answers that you need right now, Sug. I have battled this all week and I came here tonight because I need you, you've come to mean so much to me. I don't want to think about the trip that I need to make tomorrow, I just want to lay here and hold you." Joshua admitted.

CHAPTER 14

*C*arla was trying to be satisfied with the tiny bit of information that he provided, but this scene reminded her of a conversation that her sisters had about how men drop bomb shells of information on you after they've put it down sexually! But, she couldn't help to muse that at least the dick was good.

For the remainder of the night, Carla and Joshua discussed everything except Pennsylvania. She was still uneasy about the limited information that he offered, but decided to implement the benefit of the doubt rule.

Friday's class was successful. Carla grabbed her belongings for the day and headed back to her suite. She had seen Joshua off that morning after he confessed that he had clothes packed in his truck. Spending the night locked in each other's arms with Carla deciding that she could use some farewell lovemaking at two in the morning. She missed him already, but it would only be a couple more days.

Joshua had texted her when he made it to his destination, but she hadn't heard anything else from him and Carla promised herself that she wouldn't bug him.

Walking down the long hallway leading to the confinements of her home, she swiped the magnetic key and entered into the suite. The cleaning service had come and gone; cleaning the kitchen, bathroom, making the bed and situating the furniture in the living room.

Taking off her shoes, Carla planned to dispose of her clothes and wrap her hair, until she heard a knock at the entry. Grumbling all the way to the door, she checked the peephole and couldn't make out the unfamiliar faces. Carla slightly opened the door for a view and her mouth damn near hit the floor.

The first girl spoke. "Hi, are you Carla Williams?" It was the daughter with the major sex appeal and the alluring voice that Carla had researched several days before.

"I am and you must be Jasmine Williams!" Carla verified.

Smiling, "I see you've done your homework. I am Jasmine and this is my sister Jayla Williams!"

Carla opened the door wider so that they could come in. Jasmine's graceful poise that Carla never mastered, swept and enveloped the room while Jayla's presence paled in comparison to her youngest sisters. There was no mistaking that they had come from two different mothers and separate environments. "I don't know if your father mentioned it, but he left for Pennsylvania this morning!"

Smacking her lips, Jayla commented. "He's always on some extra shit! I should have known something was up when he didn't answer his phone all morning. But, since he gave us your hotel information as a backup, we decided to just take the chance."

"He left my hotel information?" Carla questioned.

Jasmine answered, "Yeah, he said that if he wasn't home, then we could find him here. Not to mention that this is a lovely hotel suite."

Carla could tell off the back that Jasmine had very expensive taste and her wardrobe preceded her. "Well you guys are more than welcome to hang here for the night, but he won't be back until Sunday!" For the first time, Carla noticed Jasmine's growing pudge.

Shrugging their shoulders, the girls telepathically communicated that they would stay. Jasmine was the first one to speak up again, "Well if we're going to stay then we're going to have to order some food because I'm starving."

"Your father didn't tell me that you were pregnant!" Carla stated.

Snickering, "That's because he doesn't know, I came to surprise him, but it looks like we're the ones who got surprised!"

"Do you mean because he's not here or because I opened the door and I'm the same age as you?" Carla needed clarity.

Both girls laughed. "His old, slick ass told us how old you were and your concern regarding how we would look at the situation, but don't worry, we know how our father can be! He usually gets what he wants."

Trying to change the subject, "Well what do you guys want to eat?" Carla reached over on the counter to grab her tablet and cell phone.

While the girls discussed dinner arrangements, Carla texted Joshua, asking if he accidentally or intentionally forgot to tell his daughters that he had left town. Placing the phone back down on the counter, she noticed the girl's discussion had stopped. "What's the matter?"

Jayla who obviously wasn't a big talker commented, "Nothing, we decided on Pizza Papalis Chicago Style."

"Okay, so do you guys want to eat in or go out?" Carla asked.

"We're tired from the drive from Virginia. So we can order the pizza and a movie and bask in a little bit of girl talk!" Jasmine smiled eagerly.

"Sure, sounds good to me." Carla reached over and grabbed her tablet to find the nearest location that would deliver and placed the call.

Carla was glad the girls resolved to the sofa to relax because her mind continued to drift to last night's events with Joshua. She was trying not to be worried and distracted that he still hadn't replied to her message that was sent two hours prior.

There were a few deep dish slices of pizza left, but the movie, *"Act like a lady, think like a Man"* had just begun rolling in the credits when Jasmine asked. "So you love my daddy, huh?"

Completely caught off guard, Carla looked like a deer in headlights. She figured the truth was her only option, but sometimes she hated the fact that she wasn't a good liar, "I do love your father!"

"I love my baby's father too, but I'm learning that no matter who the man is and what you may represent to him, he's still a man at the end of the day."

"I can agree with that, but elaborate on what you mean!" Carla was wise for her age and she had been through too much not to have learned from her lessons.

"I mean that my baby father loves me, provides for me and takes care of me, but that doesn't stop him from dipping his dick off in other females." Jasmine clarified.

Carla knew this was going to make or break their unspoken relationship, but she had to ask her. "Jasmine do you think his level of respect for you has anything to do with the fact that you were a Porn Star?"

The room was quiet enough to hear a pin drop until Jasmine found her voice, "Who told you about that? Did my father tell you about that?"

Sensing Jasmine build a wall just as Carla had watched their father do countless times. "I wasn't under the impression that your father knew about it because he doesn't watch porn. I, on the other hand, recognized your face when I looked you up on Facebook, but didn't place it until I was going through my healthy collection of adult entertainment."

"Well it definitely wasn't one of his proudest moments of me." Jasmine responded.

"And I'm not here judging, I was simply asking. Sometimes men look at our past and where we've come from and uses it as a weapon to size us up and/or use it against us. Hence, him creeping around because he knows that you're use to sharing dick." Carla lifted her hand, "Definitely No Offense!"

"None taken!" Jasmine confirmed.

Speaking up for the first time since the movie started, Jayla cut into Carla. "So what else do you know about us? I think we should put all the cards on the table; I don't like to beat around the bush. And I'm not going to sit here and play the 'let's get to know Joshua's youth' when you already seem to already know a shitload about us."

Carla thought Jayla was quiet, but she wasn't, she was Joshua, a complete replica of his personality. Jayla was observant and direct. "I know that you and your twin brother have a criminal record for boosting, but you've seemed to have turned your lives around."

Turning towards Jasmine, Carla continued. "I also know that some ratchet ass female is harassing you on

Facebook and Instagram about how your man fucks her and then comes home to you. That the tramp wonders if you know what her pussy tastes like on the tip of his dick and how you're too pretty to put up with his shit." Carla raised her hand again, "Which I agree, but that's none of my business."

Jayla sat back on the couch and crossed her legs and Jasmine decided to defend herself. "You do know that my daddy is that same kind of nicca and although he may love you, there's no guarantee that he's going to do right by you!"

Composing herself after the blow Jasmine tried to render, Carla spoke. "I already said that I'm not here to offend anyone and honestly you don't have to explain anything to me. I'm conscious of the information that I have because I don't allow people to feed me data. I search for the details myself and I'm aware of who your father is. And at any point if I feel like I can't handle it or the cross that he carries, I'll be the first one to disconnect myself!"

"So, how do you know I have a record?" Jayla inquired and back peddled in the conversation.

"Its public information if you look in the right places!" Carla wasn't going to tell her that her youngest sister Chrissey was an expert on uncovering criminals and their records. Chrissey led her to the fountain of truth and Carla drank from it.

The girls let the discussion die down and Jasmine was the first one sleep. Carla turned on another movie and Jayla watched it in silence. Jayla only moved for more to eat and to use the restroom, Carla observed that she was the anti-social one of the two.

Carla assumed she was the next one asleep; initially she worried about Jayla stealing something from her because she walked with this sneakiness in her glare. But at the end of the day, her father would repay for anything missing. It definitely was not worth missing any sleep for.

CHAPTER 15

$\mathcal{W}$aking the next morning, Carla glanced at her phone, she didn't have any missed calls or any awaiting text messages. For somebody who needed her two days ago, Joshua was sure acting as if he didn't know her now. But, she wouldn't jump to conclusions; he hadn't returned his daughters call either.

Carla saw Jasmine and Jayla off to their cars, hoping that she would see them again in the near future. Carla stretched across her bed, trying not to be edgy when the Rick Ross ring tone began playing again. The irritation that had consumed her all morning was held at bay while she answered to see what her sister wanted.

"Hey Bay Bay!" Trying to camouflage how she actually felt at that moment.

"Why does it sound like you just ran over your dog?" Chrissey inquired.

Laughing at Chrissey's inability to be tactful, "Nothing, I'm alright what's up with you?"

Bypassing her question, Chrissey continued, "What do you have up your sleeve to do this weekend?"

"I don't have any plans at the moment, I thought about coming home, but I don't know!"

"Aww, Yaay, okay we're on our way!"

"Huh? Who?" Carla's excitement escalated.

"Ebony, Morgan and I are on the road, we will be there in about two hours. We're about to pave the streets of downtown Chicago, it's going down sis!"

Smiling with tears in her eyes, "I can't wait, I'll text you the address of the hotel." Pausing. "I can't wait to see you guys!" Carla added again.

At that moment Carla said a silent prayer of thanks to God because no matter how far she strayed away from him, she was more than confident that God never left her side. No one could convince her that he hadn't sent her sisters to her rescue and for that she was grateful.

When the knock came at the door two and half hours later, Carla didn't have to guess who the guests were. Swinging open the door, she found her three favorite people standing at her threshold. Jumping on them and throwing her arms around all three before they could come inside and squealing at the top of her lungs. "God, I missed yall!"

"Damn Bay Bay, you acting like you won the lottery or something!" Chrissey couldn't help, but observe.

"Your ass is ignorant dude. I just needed y'all that's it." Carla's motto was that, you didn't need friends when you had sisters.

"Where is that nice piece of ass that you brought home?" Chrissey asked.

Morgan chimed in, "Damn Chrissey, you're going to get us put out and we've only been here five minutes."

"Thanks Morgan, Chrissey acts like she doesn't have any home training." Carla rolled her eyes.

"I was only joking, where is that nice piece of ass that I know has spread you like an eagle by now?" Morgan laughed.

"Ebony please tell me, you have some kind of sense unlike the other stooges?" Carla ignored Morgan and turned towards her sister.

"Hell naw, I'm just as ignorant as they are. We need to know if the man gave you some act right because the way your mood swings were set up, we thought about selling you like Joseph and the coat of many colors from the bible."

Carla laughed because she knew she was a piece of work, but she couldn't have been that bad. "Ha. Whatever. So what do you guys want to do first?"

Picking up on the fact that Carla eluded the question, Morgan helped her switch the subject. "I think that we could just call it a girl's night in today because it's getting late and we just got off the road. I think pizza, chicken, drinks and a chick flick are in order."

With a little bit of wine in their systems and a belly full of Chicago Style Pizza, the open forum began with Morgan. "So I don't think I want to be married!"

The room was silent and she had everyone's attention, so Morgan carried on. "I don't think I want that kind of commitment anymore. The relationship I have with Brandon is tired, repetitive and unfulfilling." Inhaling a mouthful of air and going in for the kill, "I think I want to test the waters a little bit more!" Morgan confessed.

"What the hell does testing the waters consist of?" Carla couldn't resist asking.

"This discussion is not about interrogation Carla, just let her speak her peace. You got married before you were completely ready and look what happened!" Chrissey exclaimed.

"Uh hold on hoe—." Carla went to defend herself and Ebony cut her off.

"Ivan can't have kids!"

"Whhhat?" Everyone chorused.

There was an unspoken rule that no one ever mentioned the fact that Amber was not Ivan's biological daughter. He had been there for Ebony and Amber in ways that most biological fathers weren't in traditional households.

"So what are you guys going to do?" Chrissey asked first.

"I thought you said no interrogation?" Carla corrected.

Cutting her eyes at Carla was Chrissey's only response.

Pausing to gather the strength Carla needed to come clean, since she was the next one to share. "Yes, I screwed the old man and he went out of town yesterday and I haven't heard from him since."

It seemed as if there were more than three pair of eyes on her. "And I swallowed!"

Chrissey broke the silence with giggles. "That's my girl; I knew I taught you better than that patty cake shit you were doing with Dre!"

Rolling her eyes in response to Chrissey's amusement. "Okay, so what news do you have to reveal?" Carla diverted her attention solely to Chrissey.

Tapping the tip of her chin, "I'm still getting laid on a regular basis. I still don't do commitments. I don't want to get married and we all know that I'm not having any children." Chrissey looked around, "Yep, everything's still the same with me!"

"You're ignorant dude." Morgan told Chrissey with a gurgle.

"Carla there is one other thing." Chrissey pointed her finger in the air to give the impression that she remembered her thought. "I got a speeding ticket and I had to use your name because you know my license is still suspended."

Everyone laughed, except Carla. "That shit isn't funny, I'm going to kill you Chrissey, damn man!" Launching in her direction, Chrissey took off running around the room in an attempt to escape Carla's wrath. No one knew better than Chrissey that her sister was capable of bodily harm and since the age of ten and twelve years old, she tested the theory to no end. Chrissey had more bruises and scratches from Carla than she accumulated through her past life of a tomboy.

October 1, 2012

Despite the run-in with Chrissey, Carla deemed the time with her sisters to be exactly what she needed. She had returned to work with one month left of her assignment and not one call or text message from Joshua. To say that she was devastated was an understatement; she had pulled away from her co-workers, stopped answering her family member's calls and retreated to her hotel suite every chance that she could. Carla would ride pass Joshua's house and sit in the driveway praying that he would pull up or answer the door if she knocked.

But to no avail, November 3, 2012 had arrived and her phone was silent. When Carla put the last suitcase in her truck and waited at the checkout desk to return her room key, her phone chimed. Carla's initial reaction was to ignore it because she was sure that it was her husband. But, oddly she felt a pull to check the message.

The text from Joshua read:

> *If I could be with you physically, emotionally and soulcially, I would!*

If I could love you the way that you need, then
I would!
If I could allow you to love me the way that you
want, I would!
But unfortunately Sug, right now, I can't!
Texting as fast as she could to reply:
What does this mean?
When he didn't reply she sent a second
message.
Please don't do this!

Waiting ten more minutes, Carla knew that somehow she was going to lose the battle, but she couldn't give up the war. The third message she sent was the last and final plea with tears streaming down her face.

Please talk to me.

PART 2

The Change Up

CHAPTER 16

March 22, 2013

"*Pooty* don't look like that." Kylie tried comforting her because she could tell that the pain was extremely real and the hurt went deep.

Before Carla knew it or could prevent it, fresh tears had returned and she couldn't help but reprimand herself because she had been working on this. Carla had put her sappy ass feelings in check and here this jackass came, reopening wounds that she tried to self medicate.

"Do you know I went to Pennsylvania when I couldn't get in touch with him?" Carla tried to calm herself, choking back a sob.

"You did what Pooty?" Kylie straightened.

"Yes, before I drove back to Michigan after my job assignment was over. I stopped in Pittsburgh for a few days."

Looking at the expression on Kylie's face, Carla smacked. "Don't you dare give me that parental guidance face."

"Carla are you crazy? He could have had you arrested for harassment." Kylie asked concerned.

"I'm not afraid of him and maybe a few days in jail may have been exactly what I needed because I sort of flattened the two tires on the driver's side of the car as well." Wishing that she felt some remorse about her behavior, but she didn't.

Carla silently rationalized; *Men do malicious shit to women all the time and get away with it. Joshua made me believe that he cared and loved me and then disappeared without a trace or thought.*

Kylie chimed into Carla's thoughts. "I believe the more important question is, how did you get the woman's address in PA?"

Carla drummed her fingers on her chin to decipher how she wanted to answer the question. "I searched her name under Google and then I paid for the information that they had in the database for her."

"I think you've officially lost your mind. So you drove all the way to PA, just to stalk the lady's house and flatten Joshua's tires? Did you do anything else that I should be aware of?" Kylie silently pleaded that Carla hadn't.

"Nothing that I'm willing to openly confess at this time!" Carla confirmed.

"Okay Pooty, I'm ready to pray now!" Kylie reached for Carla's hand, but Carla snatched it away.

"I'm not ready to pray about it yet, Kylie! I'm still mad as hell and when he shows his face tomorrow, I need to make a conscious decision that I won't bury him in the backyard next to the dog."

Kylie conceded. "Okay, so now what? He showed up out of the blue after all this time, what are you going to do?" Kylie's brain was in over-drive with all of this hidden information Carla provided.

"I'm not sure; he said he's coming to get me tomorrow and I'm going to let him explain."

"So you are going to hear him out?"

"I didn't reply, he just made his plea and left."

"He's pretty ballsy!" Kylie stated confidently.

"I think at this point he's hopeful, it wasn't what he said earlier, it was his eyes when he was wiping my tears and when he placed his forehead against mine. Emotionally, I think he's still just as open."

Kylie remained silent so Carla continued. "I have the rest of the night to try and sleep off some of my susceptibility so I'll be more on guard tomorrow and not so defenseless. But, he melts me like this and I remain silent because it helps shield it."

Shaking her head, Kylie resolved, "Alright Pooty, well if you need me, call me. I have to meet the boys at the house; it looks like Joshua has some splaining to do, Lucy!" Sharing a laugh, Kylie made her way to Carla's front door.

"I'll let you know how things pan out and thanks for coming to check on me and for listening." Carla hugged and kissed Kylie's cheek.

Reaching for the door Carla paused at the figure standing on the outside of the screen. Kylie stepped around her and whispered. "Looks like he came to splain early Lucy." Snickering, "Bye Pooty."

If it were any other person, Carla would have wondered how Kylie verified the identity of the man standing in her doorway, but silently she knew Kylie saw his face in the vision. And Carla speculated that Kylie knew he was going to show up before tomorrow morning.

Kylie greeted him politely while maneuvering around Joshua and down the steps towards her car. Carla's eyes followed Kylie's every move; she figured that she was safe as long as she didn't have to look at him.

When their eyes connected, Carla found her voice. "What are you doing here?"

Moving towards the opening of the door, Joshua explained. "I didn't want to wait until tomorrow; I think I've harbored this long enough."

Carla felt her temper slowly rising because of the weight from the last five months and all that she had endured. It also didn't help that she revisited the story of her and Joshua with Kylie moments before. "You didn't seem to give two shits a few months ago and it didn't stop you from blocking me on Facebook and Twitter. Or, ordering your service provider to restrict your phone from receiving incoming calls and then ultimately disconnecting the line."

"There was just something's that I couldn't explain at the time and I couldn't deal with you and all of the other circumstances that I had going on!"

"You mean like that baby?" Carla questioned.

With his face hardening, Joshua had come to Michigan to lay his burdens at her feet, but Carla already knew. "Huh?" Joshua asked pretending to be confused.

"Please don't fucking play with me, I'm so ready to fight you!" Carla warned.

"Okay, so you know about my daughter!" Joshua confirmed.

"Know about your daughter? Dude, I know about all of your kids and the poor excuse of a father that you were."

"Excuse you?" Joshua stepped closer.

"You're excused. Who did you think I was? Did you expect me to sit around and wait for you to give me closure, or fill the hole that you left?" Carla didn't give him an opportunity to chime in or explain. "You should have known better! I told you what I was capable of and how I operated once I was determined to get answers." Carla waved her arms in the air to get her point cross. "I refuse to be a victim to men that think their actions have no repercussions. I'm sure you thought you were in the clear because I was silent!"

"You're right I should have known better than to fucking make a deal with the devil on a chick like you, then crawl into your bed with a false expectation that I could walk away feeling nothing!"

"Whoa, make a deal with the devil on me?" Carla paused.

"Listen little girl, I was a player way before I became a grown man, I told you that. And there is no way that I don't get what I want, but I didn't count on loving you. I didn't count on opening up to you."

"Bullshit! Tell me about the deal?" Carla spat.

"That shit doesn't matter CeCe!" The slither in his tongue dialed down a bit. Joshua hadn't meant to mention the bet, but she roiled him up and he lost control.

She watched him step back so she came out of the door and stood on the porch. "No it matters, you were talking big shit minutes ago, don't back down now."

"Girl, you know what . . . ?" Joshua began walking towards the stairs to leave as Kylie had done minutes before.

Noticing that Joshua had dismissed her without another word, she figured she ought to go for the juggler. "Go ahead and leave, that's what you're good at, that's what you do, that's who you—."

Joshua had turned around, raced back up the steps and pushed her into the front door, snatching the words out of her mouth. "Do you think I wanted to leave you? Do you? Do you think after making love with you, burying my secrets and fears inside of you that I wanted to leave you Carla? That I wanted to walk away with the risk that you wouldn't be here when I came back?"

Sitting there silent and numb, Carla was trying to gather her thoughts, but her mind was whirling; she wanted to be pissed, she wanted to be upset, but something inside of her just couldn't. So she listened to him explain.

Moving into the house and sitting on the couch to resume the speech Joshua had been practicing for weeks. "Sug, I left to go back to Pennsylvania because my ex's sister Breanne came to visit me." Pausing to let the first piece of information settle in. "Do you remember the week you insisted that I was being weird? She showed up the night that I cancelled our date." Joshua took a deep breath. "Supposedly, my ex waited until the end of the pregnancy to tell me that she'd gotten pregnant before we broke up. She wanted to be sure that she would be able to carry the baby because at thirty-nine years of age, she was considered high risk. I left to attend the baby shower and to talk to her."

"You're talking about Vanessa?" Carla tried to get clarity.

Joshua was a man who respected his privacy as well as others and part of the reason why he didn't open up to people was because he didn't deal in exchanging information. "How do you know her name? Who are you Google Williams now?"

Carla squared her shoulders and crouched down so that they were eye-level since Joshua remained seated. "Who do you think hacked into your Facebook account? It for damn sure wasn't the FBI or the CIA."

Leaning back on the sofa, Joshua rubbed his hand over his beard as he recalled the twenty-four hours when he was locked out of his Gmail and Facebook account. "You do understand that it's a federal offense to enter into someone's email?"

"I know what the fuck it is, but it should also be a crime to walk out on someone who loves you. Leaving them crying and sobbing because the hurt and pain cuts deep and without any reasoning or explanation, just speculation. While you went on, not giving a fuck if they lived or died as you ignored the begging and pleading that was left on your voicemail. Not to mention the unanswered calls and text messages that date back as far as the day you left."

"So excuse me if I lost it." Carla continued. "If I was irrational in my attempts to find resolution. But, if you could feel the hurt and pain that I carried around for months wondering what I had done for you leave me, maybe you could sympathize. I went through every moment and memory that I had of you, trying to pinpoint where we went wrong. And contemplating if you were real or if I had conjured you up?" Carla sobbed.

Joshua didn't know what to think of the situation that money and greed had placed him in, but he had no choice, but to give her the truth and see what it afforded him. "Do you know what your husband does for a living?"

"Ex-husband." She corrected.

"Since when?" He posed.

"Since you left! I thought about re-considering once I saw that you had fathered another baby, but it didn't make me love you any less."

Rubbing the temples of his head, Joshua felt that Carla was making this harder than it needed to be. "We buried the baby four months ago, Sug." It didn't matter how many times he said it or pushed his baby girl to the back of his mind, the pain was still present.

"What do you mean you buried her?" Carla asked confused.

"The Baby Shower never took place because by the time I got to Vanessa, she had been rushed to the hospital and prepped for an emergency C-Section. The baby lived a couple days before her heart gave out. She had a Ventricular Septal Defect (VSD)."

Looking at the puzzled expression on Carla's face, Joshua elaborated. "It's a large hole in the heart where the blood is not flowing properly through the body. The doctors weren't able to detect it and it caused heart failure along with the fact that she wasn't full term yet."

The silence had begun to consume her, she had to say something. "Babe, I don't know what to say. I honestly couldn't image how you or Vanessa feel!" Joining him on the couch, Carla encircled her arms around him. She wasn't disappointed when Joshua returned the hug and buried his face in between her shoulder and neckline as he had done many times before. But, the sentimental moment dissolved when Joshua's hand began to travel up and down her body.

"Please don't do that!" Carla tried to grab his hand, almost out of breath from the desire.

Joshua inhaled her scent. "You have no idea how much I've missed you, craved you." Lifting his head with his eyes fixed on her lips.

In a perfect world Carla didn't have a right to ask or inquire about what he conducted outside of her presence, but she couldn't help the tinge of jealousy that surfaced at the thought.

"I need to know if you used your well endowed, God-gifted anatomy to console Vanessa?"

Extracting his hand from around her waist, Joshua looked at Carla as if she had lost her mind. "Did I come in here questioning you about who you've been with?" Joshua asked defensively.

"No, but it wouldn't matter because I haven't been with anyone! So your question and the discussion would have been moot."

"That's a lie and you know it!" Joshua charged.

Turning her face in disgust, "Do I look like a whore to you?"

Joshua jumped off the couch to distance himself. "I hear what your mouth is saying, but your ass and hips are much wider than they were the last time I was inside of you. Nothing, but some dick has you spread out like that because a dildo doesn't stand a chance." Joshua insulted.

Instantaneously, all of the blood drained from Carla's face, replacing it with pure fire! She couldn't decide if she should be the bigger person and escort Joshua to the door. Or, excuse herself to go in search of her gun and wear his rude ass out with the butt of it. Carla hadn't been to the gun range in months and she was dying to relieve some stress.

Instead of resulting to violence Carla was going to use a different approach. She moved off of the couch and closed the distance between them. Carla reached for both of Joshua's hands and placed one on each side of her hip. With softened eyes she whispered so calmly that it shook her. "My hips have spread because the seed that you left inside of me refuses to stop growing!"

Snatching his hands and stepping back with a quiet storm broiling in his eyes. "That's some low shit for you to claim to be pregnant, knowing that I just buried a child."

"Do you honestly believe that I would lie about a baby?"

"Carla you would have to be at least five months pregnant!"

Amused with his quick calculations, Carla reaffirmed. "I am five months pregnant Daddy and it's a boy!"

Joshua's fury escalated. "You aren't pregnant and you for damn sure aren't five months, I know what five months pregnant looks like."

"Excuse you? Are you trying to intentionally piss me off? Are you trying to make me blow this bitch up with you still in it?" Carla raged.

"There's no way in hell that I'm raising another son! So I don't know what you're going to do. I made a promise to myself not to have any more children, let alone another son." Joshua informed her.

Yelling at the top of her lungs, "Got Dammit, you don't get to make gender calls and if you would keep your dick in your pants, I assure you that these little bald headed ass babies would stop surfacing."

Carla hadn't noticed the deadliness that Joshua possessed in his walk before. "You're walking on thin ice Babygirl, so I would tread lightly if I were you."

Carla had never been the one to take threats lightly and she was the rowdiest out of all of her sisters, but she was more than hormonal, she was livid with Joshua. But, she knew that this next gut punch would have to be rendered as subtle as possible. "Just because your son Jonathan has identity issues doesn't mean that my son will."

"What the fuck did you just say?" Joshua questioned harshly.

Carla exhaled. "I know that he likes to wear women's clothing." Pausing to gather her thoughts and to give Joshua a chance to stop her, but he didn't so she continued. "I also know that he wears wigs, sew-in's and make-up. From my understanding of the description, Jonathan is a drag queen, a transvestite!"

Joshua balled up his fist, trying to calm his composure, but he was failing with every attempt. He grabbed the nearest ornament that decorated Carla's coffee table and threw it at the wall. With every bit of anger that he could muster it left a hole the size of his hand as the evidence. "Do you know what pisses me off the most about you?" He peddled forward without any indication that he expected her to answer the question.

"You found the time to dig into every aspect of my life, but you are oblivious and naïve about the bullshit that's right under your nose. You married a man and had no clue of the pull or power that he possessed. So tell me, did your nosey ass know that your husband hired me to distract you, to pull you in and then leave you? Dre wanted you back so bad that he paid me $500,000.00 to ensure that you would return back to him as damaged goods! He wanted the break to be so detrimental that you wouldn't be able to function without him and he could be the one to mend and nurse you back to health."

"What? That doesn't even make sense. He didn't know anything about the merger or even that our paths would cross!" Carla informed Joshua.

"For you to be so intelligent, you are quite adolescent. He headed the damn merger; he owns shares in the corporation that you work for. Dre approached me way before there was any talk of a merger."

Numb to the revelation, Carla calmly asked. "So who are you? Do you actually work for the corporation or is this all a scam?"

"I'm known as Ice!"

"What is that an acronym?"

"No. It's a name that I adapted because of my ability to be cold, unattached and unaffected by anyone or anything. Until I met you."

"Sounds heartless." Carla bypassed his last confession.

"It's smart, that's what it is. And I have never fallen for an assignment in the active fifteen years of this occupation."

Closing her eyes, to stop her hands from shaking, Carla asked. "And what exactly is your occupation?"

"I'm currently the head trainer at your bank, but in my past life I was a male escort." Joshua admitted.

"You mean a male prostitute?" Carla corrected.

"No, I said a male escort."

"Please elaborate on what the difference is between the two." Carla crossed her legs and interlocked her arms.

"The difference is that I don't stand on a corner, strung out on drugs with my dick in my hand."

"If this was about an assignment and money, then why fuck me? You could have done your job without including sex.

"I slept with you because he doesn't deserve you! And at the time, I needed you."

"Excuse me? But, you deserve me?"

"No, I don't deserve you either. But, I could have stayed in Pennsylvania with Vanessa. I came back for you. I loved you enough to be monogamous in the bedroom unlike your husband."

Sitting back on the cushions of the couch to become more comfortable as the baby began to push down on her bladder. "Was that a cheap shot?" Carla registered.

"No Carla, it was the truth! He doesn't respect you and he doesn't really want you. But, he understands your value and doesn't want anyone else to have you."

Rolling her eyes in the top of her head, Carla tried to clarify. "Hmm, more of your psychology? So, let me guess. You guys discussed this over tea while you were planning on how to strategically seduce and deceive me?"

"No I concluded this when I realized that my daughter Jasmine orchestrated this scheme. And then again, when Jasmine revealed that Andre is the father of her unborn child."

Carla began to think back on her initial encounter with Jasmine at her hotel room in Chicago and the baby bump that she noticed shortly after the introductions.

Propping up on the sofa, Carla felt a wave of nausea sweep over her. She couldn't help but think of how dysfunctional this whole situation was. And now she had this life growing inside of her and its Daddy was some kind of player/pimp/hoe. Along with Joshua's daughter, who was just as manipulative and deceptive.

When realization dawned on Carla that she wasn't going to be able to contain the contents of her stomach, she went in search of the bathroom. Just as she opened the lid of the toilet, the vomit spilled into the water. The wrenching became so intense that it brought her to her knees and blinded her eyes with tears. Carla hadn't noticed that Joshua entered the bathroom, let alone kneeled down behind her and wrapped his arms around her stomach to hold her and the baby.

Carla rested her head on the toilet seat and Joshua leaned his head on the side of her temple enough for his lips to touch her ears and whispered. "I'm here Baby, you're not alone." Joshua exhaled a sigh of relief as the weight of his secrets had been released. "You can count on me; we'll figure it out together." Joshua reassured.

Stifling tears and trying to wipe the snot from her nose, "I nor this baby need you, please leave!" Carla didn't have the strength to fight or to yell anymore and she wasn't going to put her pregnancy at risk to do so.

Feeling the baby move underneath his fingers for the first time. "I'm not leaving now Carla, it's too late. Don't you get what happened? This was never supposed to be!" Joshua tightened his grip on her waistline. "I wasn't supposed to love you and you weren't supposed to dig into my life and tear down every wall that I've built." He placed his nose in the crook of her neck. "You divorced Dre instead of going back to him; he's not just going to let that go. There are repercussions for that and I won't put you or this baby in anymore danger." Joshua took a deep breath and mumbled. "Sug, we've officially changed the game."

EPILOGUE

Sitting in the driver's seat of his 760 Li BMW, Andre listened to the voicemail that Ice left. He pressed the button 1 several times for it to replay until he could make sense of the foolishness.

He tried not to be extremely pissed, but his temperature was escalating. He should have known better than to send a senior citizen to do a man's job. There was no way in hell that he expected Ice to fall prey to Carla's charm. But, who was he kidding, he knew the effect that she could have on any man and that was why he wouldn't let her go.

Dre was the first man to taste and touch her and even after the separation, he ensured that he remained the only. Closing his eyes and clenching his fist at the thought of Ice being inside of her and the look of satisfaction on Carla's face. Not only did Dre want his money back, but he would make certain that there were repercussions for the disrespect shown towards him.

"Got Dammit!" Dre punched the steering wheel. He didn't have a plan B in case the mission failed. Joshua was a professional, a businessman and failure had not been an option at the time of negotiation. Leaning back against the headrest and draping his arm over his forehead, Dre tried to gather his thoughts and take a deep breath. He needed to take a step back and re-evaluate the situation to plan his next move.

Ice would pay for his inability to perform well on his promise. All a man had was his word and Ice's had returned void. Andre had questions and he expected answers, even if it was at the expense of innocent casualties.

Adjusting his seat, mirror and buckling his seat belt, Dre pulled the black beauty from the curb of Carla's townhouse. He wasn't a killer, but when it came to love there were no limits.

Coming Soon
To Know Me Is To Love Me But, Can You Handle The Real Me?

Chrissey Williams is not only the youngest of the Williams girls, but she has experienced the most; she's known as the wild child. Her pedigree resides in the church, but gravity keeps her pulled towards the streets. She has inherited her ability to hustle and grind, but her expensive taste and lust for life leads her down some valley's and constant brushes with death. It's easy to pretend that she's just a preacher's kid with flawless skin, a Porn star's body and a smile that's so inviting. Yet, inside she's fighting the battle of her life and the devil is playing for keeps.

The only way for her to survive is to keep it moving; no feelings or permanent attachments because love may get you killed. Love happens to be nothing more than extra baggage that makes you irrational, emotional and territorial. But, what will Chrissey do, when something unexpected causes her to rethink every decision she's made the last ten years? Can her sister's save her from herself or will she become the ultimate sacrifice?

Also

<u>*When love isn't enough*</u>
"When two wrongs don't make a right,
then you find an alternate route!"

It's rare, but not impossible for people to find their soul mates at a young age. It's actually more common for one person to be endlessly in love with another, but they are oblivious to the attraction.

Myah and Lance have never gotten along, in fact, they've argued the last 24 years. But, when a family crisis brings them back together; will they deal with the tension between them or will the family continue to play referee?